THE LAST GOODIE

THE
LAST
GOODIE

STEPHEN SCHWANDT

Holt, Rinehart and Winston
New York

Copyright © 1985 by Stephen Schwandt
All rights reserved, including the right to reproduce this
book or portions thereof in any form.
Published by Holt, Rinehart and Winston,
383 Madison Avenue, New York, New York 10017.
Published simultaneously in Canada by Holt, Rinehart and
Winston of Canada, Limited.

Library of Congress Cataloging in Publication Data
Schwandt, Stephen.
The last goodie.
Summary: Haunted by the still unsolved abduction of
his babysitter twelve years ago, high school senior and
track star, Marty Oliver, stumbles on a clue that provides
a new lead in the case and finds himself involved in a
dangerous adventure.
[1. Mystery and detective stories.   2. Track and
field—Fiction]   I. Title.
PZ7.S39955Las   1985   [Fic]   85-5641
ISBN: 0-03-005182-7

First Edition

Designed by Abby Kagan
Printed in the United States of America
1   3   5   7   9   10   8   6   4   2

ISBN 0-03-005182-7

7093316

For Karen

"There are some people who cannot resist the desire to get into a cage with wild beasts and be mangled."

—Henry Miller

THE LAST GOODIE

CHAPTER ONE

Even though it was only early October, the night was cold, cold and clear with bright stars and a half moon. A vigorous and purifying bleakness. Occasionally, a random gray-black cloud scudded over the moon, and then the sky changed and looked frozen and remote and ominous. That's the way it is sometimes in Minneapolis.

She had finished reading the boy his three bedtime books and had tucked him in and had listened to his confident, well-rehearsed prayers. Before she had pulled his bedroom door closed and returned to the homework and TV downstairs, she had looked back in on him. She saw him swimming under his puffy down quilt, nearly lost in the full-sized bed, with rows of stuffed animals surrounding him, his right arm hooking his favorite pet, a light brown ducklike creature with a bright orange beak and feet, which he insisted was a "pelican"—Peter Pelican.

She smiled at him. He was wide-eyed and waiting. She always pretended she was going to leave without going through the ritual, but she always "remembered" before the boy had to remind her. She had been his only baby-sitter, and she knew him.

"Good night, Marty," she whispered back.

"Good night," he replied, articulating carefully.

"Sleep tight. Don't . . ."

"Let the . . ."

"Bugs . . ."

"Bite!" he squealed.

"And if . . ."

"They do . . ."

"Hit 'em . . ."

"With a shoe!!"

"Good night, sweetness," she said warmly, ending it as she eased the door shut, leaving it open a crack so a little bar of dim light would be there to comfort and direct him should he have to get up for anything. "Now you stay put. No more hide-and-seek, okay?"

"No?"

"No."

"I love you, Stacy," he said.

"I know. I love you too."

And she did, really. He was convinced of it. After all, she had never missed sending him cards and little presents at Christmas, on his birthday, for no reason at all sometimes.

What happened next is pure conjecture, years of it.

Perhaps she walked quietly downstairs and returned to the family room couch, where her study questions in history awaited her reluctant efforts. Perhaps she glanced at her watch and realized that in little less than an hour her father would call to check on her, as he always did, ever *since she was an eleven-year-old rookie baby-sitter. She knew she wouldn't have to deal with the phoning ritual much longer, though, because this would undoubtedly be one of her last baby-sitting jobs.*

She was getting too old, a junior in high school already. Her priorities were changing, her options increasing, her awareness of life's possibilities expanding. She was intelligent, smart in school. She was a promising runner, "an inevitable state champion," according to her well-respected, highly successful track coach at Southwestern, John Hiles. She was tall, slender, pretty, and was quickly becoming beautiful, and she was only baby-sitting tonight because she had canceled out of a date and because five-year-old Marty Oliver was her favorite client.

She couldn't have been seated more than fifteen minutes when she might have heard the first tentative rattling along the north gangway of the sedate Cape Cod house. She detected the noise only because she had turned off the TV and was reading in silence. She had tried to ignore the rattling, but it persisted, ruining her concentration. Soon she became fearful.

She switched off the table lamp next to her and walked quietly toward the kitchen, where she would try to get a look outside while checking the back door. She'd blackened the room and was nearing the kitchen when the rattling ceased. She moved through the dining area and stopped at the big window facing the backyard. When she peeked between the curtains she might have seen it, a motion, something gliding toward the house, its shadow fleeting across the blue lawn. She hurried to the back door and examined the lock. The dead bolt was closed, snapped securely shut.

Next, she pressed her face to the door glass, trying to

3

penetrate the deep shadows of the gangway and locate the source of the disturbance. She saw nothing. She was about to return to the family room and her books and the inevitable phone call when she thought she heard a creak. She stopped, held her pose, and listened.

She stood frozen to the linoleum tile of the kitchen floor, her head cocked, concentrating, listening, but hearing only the heavy, almost choking throbs of her own pounding heart. Suddenly she heard it again, a small agonizing squeal . . . creaking. She looked toward the stairs leading to the basement.

She tiptoed silently up to the darkly stained oak door at the top of the stairway and gripped the knob. Her other hand rested on the switch controlling the stairway light located behind the door. Slowly, silently, she twisted the brass handle and readied herself for . . . for what? When the door clicked free, she threw it open, snapped on the light, and screamed so loudly that the boy upstairs heard her.

"AAAAAAAAGGHHH!" she wailed.

The boy pulled the covers over his head.

"NO!! NO, JESUS!!! NO! . . . TSEE! . . . HURT!!"

Her next scream died in her throat.

Upstairs, the sleepy, disoriented boy crawled out of his bed and slid underneath it, seeking silence, peace and quiet, a place to rest, to hide. Under the bed was his secret "fort," which was populated by an entirely different set of stuffed pets. Only Peter Pelican lived in both worlds.

The boy burrowed deep into his special fort sleeping bag and dozed off, never knowing just how scared he should have been. He slept there and didn't awaken until he heard the telephone ring and ring. He listened to it for a long time, wondering why Stacy didn't answer it, why it

---
4

wouldn't stop. Finally, the rhythmic ringing hypnotized him into an even deeper sleep.

Then, just moments later, or so it seemed, his father was clutching at him, dragging him out from under the bed. His mother had been there, too, and Stacy's father. Everybody was crying, hysterical. Soon both his parents were holding him so tightly they terrified him and he began crying, knowing something horrible had happened. He thought they were mad at him for getting out of bed.

"Oh, lord!" his father had sobbed.

"Marty," his mother whispered through her tears. "Marty, Marty . . ."

It wasn't long before he found out that what everyone feared actually had happened. He listened to the conversations of policemen and neighbors as he rode around in his father's powerful, tightly closed arms, while his dad, a journalist, helped to gather information. His mother had said, "Ken, take Marty over to Sally's. He shouldn't hear this." But his father refused, and soon the boy had heard it all, how it must have been.

The "intruder" had apparently entered through the oversized basement window. He had apparently dragged Stacy down the steps when she'd opened the stairway door. Then he pulled her through a basement walkout door, which had been locked from the inside. One of her running shoes was found outside. There were bloodstains on the flagstones. Just past the window well, police discovered a bloody hand print on the side of the house.

No other significant evidence was found. No footprints, car tracks, bits of clothing—nothing. One neighbor said she thought she'd heard screaming, but on high school football nights such cries always seemed to come from drunken cel-

ebrants who spent their postgame energy racing up and down dark streets in their cars.

The little boy thought about Stacy's last screams, the very last one. Perhaps she'd been yelling at her attacker, futilely trying to ward him off, but the boy feared that her final scream was meant for him. He could still hear what she yelled, but to him it meant nothing. When he told his father about his fears, his dad replied, "She was scared, Marty. Scared and angry. So she swore."

The boy grew up. And all the while he was growing, something else was growing, too. With each passing day, month, year, it became painfully obvious that Stacy Davis would never be seen alive again, would never be found at all. And that hard-to-face fact brought on a growing guilt in the boy.

He grew up believing he should have been with her, done something to save her. He sometimes felt he didn't deserve to live if she couldn't or didn't. There must have been something he could've done. He should have been able at least to understand her last message, the strangled scream that changed her voice and, he believed, called to him, warning him, telling him. It was probably the clue to everything.

So there were nightmares. Throughout grade school he would wake up once or twice a month screaming to himself, calling for her, sitting bolt upright, waking in a sweat, hearing the rhythmic pounding echo of her last cry: "NO! . . . TSEE! . . . HURT!!"

Seconds after the boy yelled himself awake, his father and mother would be there to calm him, to assure him that no one would ever harm him, that everything was okay, that he was safe. His mother would plead with him to forget the experience. "Put it out of your mind," she said, "or it'll poison you." His father angered his mother when he'd turn on a tape recorder and talk Marty through the dream, hoping to uncover some shred of evidence that might crack what was still the area's most frustrating and frightening unsolved crime. The boy felt guilty. His father felt responsible. The sanctity of his home had been violated. Another couple's child had disappeared, might be dead. How could he not feel responsible?

And his parents suffered other ways too. For a while they had an unlisted phone number, after the crank calls got to be too much. Crazies of all ages had made threats, said they'd be back for the kid soon, tonight even. Others calmly suggested, using sarcasm like a club, that the boy himself was somehow behind everything because he was jealous of the sitter's new beau. And it got even sicker sometimes. Marty's family had considered moving, but that had been financially impossible.

Not so for the Davises. Similar phone calls drove Stacy's parents out of the neighborhood, out of the city. And after the Incident, it had been almost impossible for the boy's parents and Stacy's to see each other. Her father and mother were inconsolable, and rightly so. She was special. Everyone knew that.

Even today, over ten years later, the boy remembers her, but in a different way. Now he too runs. He runs hard to find her, to learn about her, what she must have felt when she won championships; to win the repeated championships that she was denied. He runs to exhaust his guilt and fear. But mostly he wants to finish the job she'd given him with her last plea. He searches his mind for the exact phrasing, the exact emphasis, the exact sound she'd made that night so long ago now, yet never far enough away.

"Marty!" his father called from downstairs. "If you don't get moving, we'll never make it. Marty?"

"Yeah, Dad," he hollered back.

"Well?"

"Be right there. I'm just reading something."

"Now! Get down here *now*! They won't delay a ten-team track meet just because Mr. Invincible felt like relaxing with a book."

It wasn't a book. It was an essay, a "narrative/experience exploration" he'd written at the beginning of his junior year at Southwestern for Mr. Lonsbury's creative-writing class. He'd spent two nights writing and rewriting it in a desperate attempt to meet the assignment deadline.

"There's no such thing as a late paper in this course!" Lonsbury had bellowed on the first day of class. "After the due date has passed, the assignment and you, the student writer, simply do not exist!"

Ignoring that ultimatum, Marty had put off dealing with the subject and the assignment until forty-eight hours before it was due. He remembered now, as he put the sheets back into the manila folder, that during his final all-night composition session he'd revised and revised and revised, and with each revision, with each refocusing, his memories of the trauma had clarified and intensified and magnified until he came to the point where he'd somehow actually recreated the emotional and physical distress he'd experienced as a terrified five-year-old.

While he had written, his arms and neck had tensed, and eventually slow, deep aches had begun surging, plowing down the middle of his back as he sat at the typewriter. Near the end of the writing marathon, his face had felt flushed and hot, and as he tapped out the last lines, he'd clamped his jaws so tightly shut that his grinding teeth had seemed about to shatter.

The tragedy of the project was that when he'd finished it, was satisfied with what he'd done, he had decided not to turn it in. That morning, as the drab gray skies outside his second-floor bedroom window had become pink with dawn, Marty concluded that the narrative was too personal, too important to let go of, to reveal. Even to his mother—to her especially. At school he'd sought and received an unheard-of extension. "Just once I'll let you break the rule I gave you, Martin," Lonsbury had said, "if what you write is good, and if it works."

Instead of the kidnapping story, then, Marty turned in a day-late narrative about a sailboat race. He'd been penalized half a grade for tardiness. Marty took the A − in full stride and with a smile.

"Martin!!" his father called again.

"Okay!"

"Hey listen, we gotta *go*! It's deadline time!"

C H A P T E R

TWO

They drove with the windows down in the full-sized Buick sedan so the warm, sweet afternoon air of late May could swirl through the car and refresh them. The trip to the Southwestern High School stadium was a short and pleasant one, a drive that took them through stately neighborhoods of colonial, Cape Cod, and Victorian homes set back from streets lined with cathedrally arched elm trees.

They would make it to the school in plenty of time for Marty to change clothes and join his teammates in warm-ups. As they eased along, Marty knew his father was as anxious and as excited as he himself was, because this last big invitational track meet was the final tune-up before regions. And regions, of course, were the big first step leading to the state meet, possibly to another state championship.

"What were you reading that's so important?" asked Ken Oliver, his dark, longish hair feathering in the breeze.

"Just a thing I wrote last year."

"What 'thing'?"

"That narrative/experience paper for Lonsbury. You know."

"About Stacy Davis?"

"Yeah." Marty looked out his window.

"It's funny."

"What?" Marty glanced at his father.

"In the spring, each track season, I think about her more than usual, too."

Marty nodded, said nothing.

"Is there any reason beyond the obvious why you'd look at that essay now?"

"What's 'the obvious'?"

"I don't know. I guess you'd obviously reread it if you were bothered by that business again."

Marty thought a moment and then said, "Maybe it's because everything's ending. Track is ending. High school is ending."

"Isn't that the truth."

"I meant, it's ending for me, personally."

"You and everybody else in your class, personally. Everybody in the place."

Marty laughed. "I guess you're right. No more Southwestern High for anybody after this year."

"Let's hear it for financial planning, huh? Fiscal responsibility."

"That's part of it, too, probably a big part—the school closing." Marty paused, reflected. "Anyway," he continued, "I just want to clean things up, you know? I want to tie up all the loose ends and go out in style."

As they pulled into the high school parking lot, and the old sprawling brown-brick building commanded their attention, Marty thought about how, all his life, he'd assumed the school would just be there, forever, like trees and sidewalks, that it would always remain open and attended. But nothing was sacred this year when the unthinkable became thinkable, and the ridiculous was called inevitable. This year, schools rich in tradition and well supported by the neighborhoods they served, schools like Southwestern, whose academic and athletic achievements were notable, schools like that could be closed virtually without meaningful debate simply because some bureaucrat decided to justify his paper shuffling.

In track, guided by Coach John Hiles, Southwestern had won the state championship seven times in the last ten years, a seemingly untouchable record. And years ago, twelve years ago, a young girl runner named Stacy Davis showed such promise that John Hiles had named her girls' team captain when she was only a sophomore.

"Don't worry," Ken Oliver said, as Marty started to get out of the car. "You'll go in style. But if you don't, it won't be for lack of opportunity, right? You just have to work your way through it. Like always."

Marty assumed his father was talking about track, about the series of mile runs that lay between the present and the end—the state meet.

"Dad," said Marty as he climbed from the car, "do you still have all those old tapes?"

"Sure."

"Maybe I'll want to listen to them again, okay?"

"Sure, why not."

Marty chunked the door shut.

"Good luck," said Ken Oliver, leaning across the front seat, talking through Marty's open window.

"Thanks," Marty said, without looking back.

Marty knew his father was watching him as he jogged around to the back of the school, where he'd find an open door to the locker room. And Marty knew that after another few minutes Ken Oliver would head for the stands and, as always, climb high in the bleachers to find an unobstructed view of the games below. That was the way they always did things at home meets. That was the ritual.

The tapes Marty had mentioned were recordings of conversations he and his father had had through the years regarding the Incident. It had been typical of Ken Oliver, a thorough journalist, a popular interviewer and feature writer, to take notes whenever young Marty had awakened from a nightmare. With his tape recorder on, Ken had patiently talked the terrified boy through the specifics of the dream, trying to calm and reassure him but always hoping for that big break, that significant detail that little Marty might call up from his subconscious, the missing piece that would help them to reconstruct the story behind the still-unsolved case of Stacy Davis.

As for the tapes, there were at least forty of them covering nearly eight years of bad dreams, perhaps a hundred little conversations in all. The last time Marty had tried listening to them was the summer before his first year at Southwestern. But he'd given up quickly because recalling the experience was upsetting and because his young-boy voice and little-kid thoughts embarrassed him. Overall, he was doubtful about the value of the recordings. He'd even asked his dad to destroy them, as if the embedded fears would be erased along with his words. But his father chose to keep them. A psychologist friend had said they'd eventually prove "therapeutic." Marty's mother, on the other hand, was convinced they'd prove worthless at best. Making them, she thought, had probably been damaging and dangerous for young Marty. Keeping them was simply stupid.

Regarding his essay (or anything else he'd written), Marty knew both his father and mother were intensely interested. His parents had been told by the public school system that their son, their only child, showed "definite measurable signs of verbal giftedness," but Marty doubted the accuracy of that evaluation.

Marty, however, knew his father was indeed verbally gifted. Ken Oliver could make words do things, whatever he wanted them to do. His words made people react. He had not only risen through the ranks of Twin City journalists but had also sold long articles to national magazines. The latest of these pieces had been picked up by *Esquire*. And like most writers, Ken Oliver had attempted book-length projects, one of which was purchased and published when Marty was just starting junior high school. It was a "paperback original," a mystery about a jazz musician, a trumpet player, who killed three former girlfriends and played his horn to them as they died from poisoning. The book was called *Love Taps*, and Marty had read it and liked it. Parts of it he'd even found funny. But nothing was funny about real-life crime.

Before entering the locker room, Marty looked over at the athletic field, which was already becoming crowded with colorfully uniformed competitors. The brightness and excitement and pageantry of big invitational meets had always motivated rather than intimidated him. He'd always performed well in the showcase meets. Now he stood there wishing his mother was around to share his joy, the pure exuberance he felt at being The Man, the number-one miler

---

for this particular moment in the history of Southwestern track. By now he could understand what she had done and why she had done it, but at moments like this none of it made very good emotional sense.

It had begun a few days before Christmas. His mother announced one evening at dinner that Rachel Griffin had asked her to come down to Arizona to relax for an indefinite period of time. Rachel Griffin, twice-divorced and living in Phoenix, was still his mother's closest friend, and they'd been friends since high school. Rachel had thought Marty's mother might want to do a little painting, that she might just need a break, some time away from . . . everything.

While his mother talked that evening, Marty had watched his father's expression go from confusion to hurt. Marty said nothing when she finished, but he'd sensed that beneath the cordial, reasonable tone of his mother's words something mysterious and upsetting and important was being revealed.

"Why now?" his father had asked quietly, respectfully. "Can't you wait until after the holidays?"

"I can't," she'd replied simply.

"When?"

"The day after tomorrow."

That night she'd stopped in Marty's room and tried to talk to him alone, tried to make him understand. She'd been patient and seemingly honest in explaining her thinking and actions.

"I've got to be on my own awhile, honey," she'd said. "It's not exactly your father, and of course it's not you. It's not any one big reason. It's just that I feel sort of over-powered by our life right now.

"You and your father are so alike and so lucky at this

15

moment in your lives. You're both ambitious, driven, competitive people who have a wonderful sense of mission and purpose. You can see where you want to go and you know how to get there. You've chosen worthwhile goals and have been exactly right in discovering what it takes to achieve them. You believe in yourselves and your work. I felt like that once . . . but not anymore." She looked down at her hands, which were folded in her lap. "Well, who knows, maybe I didn't really have those feelings ever, even once. Maybe I'm just fooling myself in thinking I did. I guess that's what I have to find out."

Marty had thought then about how his mother had been victimized by the same circumstances that were now conspiring to close his high school. For nine years Carolyn Oliver had been a studio art teacher at Madison High, the toughest of the city schools. During her years there, however, the tall, trim, auburn-haired woman had not only offered ambitious and successful classes but had also won statewide recognition for her own watercolors. And along the way, she'd discovered and nurtured the talents of at least a dozen students who today were living by their art alone.

Like so many wonderfully competent teachers before her, she became a casualty of the seniority system, an approach that rewarded only longevity, not excellence, imagination, and originality. A year and a half ago, when cutbacks had been necessary, she'd lost her job to a twenty-year district veteran with a dusty teaching major in art. But he'd been in administration, out of the classroom for years. Tragically but predictably, Carolyn Oliver had been completely unsuccessful at finding another teaching job.

Instead, Marty's mother had settled for a job as a commercial illustrator. Soon, though, the unimaginative and mechanical nature of her assignments taxed her patience. She resigned after only six months. Next, she had tried her hand at display work for a major department-store chain based in Minneapolis, but found that work boring, and again quit after only a few months. Since the display/designer fiasco, she'd stayed at home and made lots of long-distance calls to Rachel Ross-Taylor-Griffin in Phoenix, Arizona.

"I guess I'm feeling a lot like some of the kids in your class, Marty," his mother continued. "I'm trying to find myself. I have to decide who I am and what I'm going to be all over again. I'm looking for a center and I'm afraid I can't find that while I'm here, caught up in a million routines. I need a change, just for a little while. A change. Can you understand what I'm trying to say?"

Marty watched as her eyes welled with tears. He had nodded, faking understanding. As soon as he realized she was actually leaving, he'd quit listening to her. Instead, he thought about himself and how deceived and betrayed and deserted he felt. All he managed to mumble was, "I think I get it." He too wondered, Why now?

"You know I love you, Marty," she'd said, walking toward the door. "Don't ever forget that. And one day you'll see that sometimes you have to do drastic and painful things to get out of the cages you let yourself slip into. You can't find your way if you're not free to look."

What cages? Marty had asked himself. Free to look for what?

After Carolyn Oliver had been in Phoenix for two weeks she called home and told her husband and son that she needed more time. She told them she was going to Mexico with Rachel Griffin to meet another friend who had a condominium on the ocean. She said that she planned to do some painting and photography and lots of thinking down there. She said she was feeling better and that Marty and his dad should think about her and pray for her.

They didn't hear from her again for almost a month, and between times Ken Oliver became worried about her safety. He made some calls himself, indiscreet, blundering inquiries. He got nowhere. When she finally did phone again, she was back in Phoenix. Marty heard his father ask his mother if he couldn't fly down to see her and talk to her. She told him not to. She said they shouldn't see each other until she was sure she was ready and the time was right.

At that moment, Marty decided to ignore anything she had to say until she came home to say it in person, face-to-face. Fortunately, he'd been able to turn the anxiety and frustration and anger he often felt toward his mother and her behavior to good use. It was just another dimension of the acute emotional edge he'd been able to maintain throughout the spring, for the entire track season. It had helped to make him *Numero Uno*, thank you, Mom.

And, ironically, during those last agonizing weeks of winter and first teasing days of spring, Marty shared with his father the plight of being alone. Shortly after his mother left his father, Marty received the Letter himself.

The previous spring Marty had dated a senior girl named Debi Donnovan, a sprinter on last year's girls' team, a bubbly dark-haired beauty. They'd maintained their relationship throughout the summer and had even remained faithful during the fall, despite Debi's being away at college in Boston. She wasn't able to fly home until her semester break at Christmas, and when Marty saw her for the first time he knew something (which is to say everything) had changed.

"Hey you look great!" Marty had opened with when he met her at the airport.

Debi had responded, "Yeah . . ."

"Really . . ."

"Um . . ."

"Well . . ."

"So . . ."

"So, do you like it?"

"What?"

"College, Boston."

"Sure. You know that."

"That's right . . . I do."

"You read anything about existentialism yet?"

"Unh-uh. That some new kinda subsistence jazzercize?"

"Funny . . ."

"I guess not."

"Not what?"

"Some new kinda—"

"Marty," she cut in, "you haven't been authentically interesting for a pretty long time, you know that?"

"Ahhh . . ."

"What's that supposed to mean?"

After only an hour with her, Marty felt so hopelessly unsophisticated and ignorant that he almost pulled the plug on their flickering flirtation right then. But he didn't. It was the only flirtation in town for him just then. Instead, he spent all the time he could with her and did his best to recapture the past.

When the Letter came shortly after her return to Boston, he realized how futile love at long distance was. So that loss, along with the departure of his mother, and his father's newfound commitment to spending "quality time" with his son—all those changes worked to bring Marty and his dad closer together, closer, in fact, than they'd ever been.

Now Marty stared at the infield full of runners and jumpers, all starting their first tentative warm-up stretches. He still didn't know what to think of his mother or his feelings toward her. His father had told him only last week that "a great deal of progress" had been made and that his mother "may be home very soon" and that "we've got to be patient with her." But his dad had said nothing since then, so Marty assumed it was just another false hope. He wondered what in the world she'd been doing all these months in Mexico and Arizona and who knows where else. He wondered and he imagined that—

"Wake up, Marty Oliver! You get your can in here, boy!"

Marty spun around and looked toward the locker-room door and saw crazy Ted Harper waving him over. Once again Harper had fooled him completely, this time with his nearly flawless Coach John Hiles impression.

CHAPTER
THREE

*T*hroughout the afternoon, at least for the boys' team, the meet followed a predictable script. Even before the mile run began, the Southwestern Salukis were well on their way to clinching another major invitational championship.

The Salukis . . .

Like other members of Southwestern's athletic teams, Marty had taken his share of kidding about the team name, the team mascot.

"Hey, Oliver, what the hell's a saluki?" rivals asked again and again, laughing, laugh-laugh, laugh, laugh, laugh . . . oh, laugh.

When Marty learned the saluki was related to the greyhound, had been bred by ancient Egyptian and Arabian nobles for endurance and speed, is considered by modern dog lovers to be a beautiful and dignified and headstrong runner, Marty joined Coach Hiles in thinking the saluki was the perfect emblem.

Now, feeling proud and formidable in his red-and-gold uniform, Marty made his courtesy rounds to the various events, stopping just long enough to encourage his teammates. He knew when his time came, they'd be lining the track, cheering him on. That was one of John Hiles's inflexible traditions: as many members of the team as possible were expected to be trackside for races of one lap or more, both relay and individual runs. Hiles always had his teams convinced that the tactic demonstrated a strong-willed unity that intimidated opponents.

Over the years, John Hiles had discovered many ways of appealing to his teams, motivating them to believe in the tactic and perform it with intensity. Considering the magnitude of his success, Coach Hiles seldom met resistance from his athletes. They all knew how much he hated the posing, the shows of detachment and indifference put on by "stars" from other schools. "If you're not running, jumping, or throwing, you damn well better be cheering!" he'd often yelled.

Marty moved through the crowded infield, his stomach muscles tightening with excitement and anticipation as he observed the spectacle of the ten-team meet. He scanned the nearly filled bleachers. He greeted challengers. And soon enough he began thinking about what he called his "focusing ritual."

About fifteen minutes before his race he would wander off by himself and close his mind to all other considerations, tunneling his vision, seeing only the track with its smooth black surface, himself running and leading, his pace and strategy unfolding, his final charge and sprint for the finish line, his crossing first and winning. He seldom thought about his competitors. Usually he'd run away from them by the second lap.

"Marty, can I talk to you a minute?" It was Coach Hiles.

Startled, Marty almost snapped to attention. "What?" Marty asked.

"Sorry to break in, but we've got a little emergency. You seen Harper?"

"Not for a while, unh-uh."

John Hiles sighed, shook his head, looked down. "Why does he persecute me like this? Haven't I done right by him this year?" Before Marty could answer, Coach Hiles started walking away. He'd gone about five steps before he turned toward Marty and said, "Get back to psyching up. But if you see Teddy, send him right to me, understand?"

"Sure." Marty sat down again. He smiled to himself. Harper. What a character. "A character with no character." That's how Bruce Skuppers, the principal of Southwestern, once described Ted Harper. Harper had been Marty's chief rival since ninth grade, the year they both started running. He'd pushed Marty to more winning finishes in the mile than he could count. They had finished one-two so often, in fact, that one local sportswriter called them "M. O. and his Shadow." From then on Harper was called "the Shadow Man" or later just "Shadow." Remarkably, they'd remained friends and committed teammates despite their intense, continuous competition.

Moreover, they had worked well together in other sports too. This past season they'd been the starting guards on Southwestern's basketball team. Most of the team's wins were credited to their fierce play on defense, their ability to press the opposition's guards all over the court for an entire game without ever seeming to tire.

And oddly, Marty and Ted looked enough alike to have been mistaken for brothers more than once. Both were dark-haired, clear-skinned, handsome boys, about the same size, a little less than six feet tall, with Harper being the "thicker" (as basketball coach Arnie Ellis once said) of the two, the one who seemed most likely to gain weight quickly should he ever quit training altogether. Beyond the superficialities of appearance, however, the differences between Ted and Marty were substantial.

Although Marty liked Ted Harper, they weren't always close friends outside school. Harper was too erratic, too unpredictable to be trusted in public . . . as a friend. He would do anything for a laugh, and too often for Marty's nerves Harper did things, strange things, just to see what would happen, how people would react. Nothing was sacred. In short, Harper seemed to relish the attention that shocking behavior got him and to disregard the consequences of that behavior.

In junior high, for example, Harper had been the first of the group to master the art of making rude noises with his moist palms and armpits, a skill he frequently displayed during reading hours, major tests, or all-school assemblies. One spring he went through a month-long phase where he responded to any friend's hello by squealing the word *groin* from the corner of his mouth.

In high school, Marty watched with amusement when Harper brought his flamboyance to varsity athletics. For instance, during an important dual meet against Southwestern's chief rival for the conference championship, sophomore miler Ted Harper failed to show up for the start of his race, his varsity debut. The event took place without him. Just before the final relay on that warm, sunny, windless Saturday, a team manager spotted Ted on the pressbox roof. Wearing only running shorts and sunglasses, Harper had retired there to work on his tan. Unfortunately, he'd fallen asleep, dozing right through the mile and most of

---

the meet. He couldn't be forgiven for following a whim and getting a little careless. He'd even brought along suntan lotion. Hiles rewarded him with a week-long suspension, and twenty extra "killer drills" on the day of his rein-statement.

As a junior, Ted pulled a stunt that ended his track sea-son early. After running his mile at the conference prelimi-naries, once again coming in second to Marty, Harper got upset because he was hungry and couldn't find anything to eat. He'd skipped breakfast and had brought no lunch, no snacks. Planning ahead had never been his forte. So to get what he wanted, he simply commandeered the team bus and drove it to a nearby McDonald's. When he returned to the meet, his stomach packed with three quarter-pounders and a chocolate shake, his "indefinite suspension" was wait-ing for him.

This year Harper was behaving much better. Marty thought Ted was trying to "work up to his potential" before he goofed all his potential away. Perhaps because this was Southwestern's last track season ever, Harper had decided to get serious. Still, he had his moments of weakness. He couldn't always resist the impulse to play, especially when temptation challenged his imagination.

It happened earlier in the season, just after the weather had turned warm. Southwestern was participating in a twelve-team meet at a beautifully landscaped, wealthy west-suburban high school, and Marty had been sitting in the stands with Harper and his girlfriend, Shari Sullivan. They were watching the sprints and hurdle races and weren't ready yet to begin warming up for their event. The three of them had found a place to sit halfway up the bleachers at about the fifty-yard line, and they were still staring silently down at the track when Shari Sullivan directed their attention to the south end of the field where the discus competition was being held on the other side of the chain-link fence.

"Why do those guys have to be inside that building when they throw?" asked Shari, her head tilted interrogatively, a long well-manicured finger resting on her flawless cheek.

At first Marty and Ted had no idea what Shari was talking about. Her nickname of "Airy" (airhead) Shari was one consequence of her sometimes offbeat but usually imaginative questions and comments. At about the same time, however, the two boys looked beyond the fence and understood what she meant. Blocking their view of the discus ring was a ten-by-ten-foot equipment shed, and from their vantage point it appeared the discus throwers were standing inside the shed, that it was a three-sided safety cage. Marty and Ted both knew the throwing circle was in front of the shed, outside it, but Ted spoke before Marty could explain.

"Geez, I don't know, Shari," Harper said thoughtfully, scratching behind his ear, his forehead lined with furrows of mock concentration. He stared squinty-eyed as discus after discus appeared to whirl out from the shed. Then Marty saw Harper wink, and he knew Ted's imagination had been stirred. "Just a sec," Harper said as he stood up. "I'll check this out."

Marty and Shari watched Ted work his way down the crowded bleachers and jog over to the discus area. They saw him talking to a guy from another school. The two of them exchanged a few sentences and then gave a hand slap.

When Harper returned to the bleachers, he sat down next to Shari, looked at her, and in a convincingly serious voice said, "You won't believe this."

"What?" she asked, unsuspiciously.

Yeah what? Marty wondered.

"Well, you realize this invitational is called the Parker Olympiad?"

"So?"

"So, you ever seen that famous statue of the Greek discus thrower? Anything peculiar about the man?"

Shari looked at Ted. Then her jaw dropped. "No," she said in a near whisper, her beautiful eyes big with comprehension.

"You got it, babe. These people, they really know how to go for authenticity."

"You don't mean—"

"Yes," interrupted Harper, "I do mean. Those boys over there are inside throwing bare-butt naked, or 'in the Greek style.' That's what the guy told me."

"I don't believe you," snapped Shari, smiling. "You're always teasing."

"Look then," said Harper, standing up, an obvious signal, for just as Ted rose to his feet and pointed to the discus area, the thrower he'd been talking to turned his back, grabbed the waistbands of his sweat pants and shorts, and dropped them to his knees, bending over, mooning boldly for a full three-count before stepping behind the shed.

"Ugh!" shrieked Shari, laughing now. She whirled to face Harper and gave him an elbow in the stomach. "You're sick, Teddy," she said, still giggling. "A case of arrested development."

"Naw."

"What'd you have to pay that guy?" Shari asked.

"Not a thing. That's Brad Boyd from Regis. I met him at a party last summer. He's goofier than I am."

"Enough said," Shari had answered, shaking her head, rolling her eyes at Marty.

The mile run, which most spectators consider the glamour event, the centerpiece of the meet, went pretty much as expected on that beautiful afternoon at Southwestern. After two laps, Marty and Ted had cut loose and were well ahead of the field, although another good runner, one of the "quality" milers Marty would compete against in regions, was keeping pace and remained within striking distance.

But when they rounded the final turn, Marty was in the lead, the loud cheers of the spectators urging him on, Shadowman Ted Harper typically trailing by two strides. As they crossed the finish line, Marty could hear Harper laughing. He always laughed at the end. He could laugh because he still had the energy to. He wasn't appropriately spent. And that was the rap against Ted. "Here's a guy," all the coaches and most of the parents would say, "who's got it all, all the tools a kid could ever want for this event— the unlimited potential to excel, to be a gifted athlete— but who'll never fulfill his promise because something's missing."

Some said he didn't have the disposition, the mental concentration necessary for long-distance running. Others said that considering his erratic, daredevil personality, he would have been happier as a sprinter, because they were, by definition, "unusual." Whatever the explanation, Ted was an enigma to his coaches, to his teammates, to his friend, Marty Oliver.

CHAPTER
FOUR

The following Monday, during his sixth and last period, Marty sat alone in Coach Hiles's office. He stared at the three battered file cabinets lining the west wall of the cubicle. Marty was Hiles's teaching assistant (T.A.) that hour, and he'd been given the job (or, in his coach's words, "honored with the responsibility") of packing all the coach's files into used yearbook boxes. The manila folders, jammed with statistics sheets, old lecture notes, hundreds of coaching and training articles, and anything else Hiles had acquired and thought worth saving during his nineteen years at Southwestern, fit perfectly into the heavy-duty, lidded cardboard boxes.

Hiles was, to say the least, depressed by the closing of his school. He once told Marty that even though, like most teachers, he'd always expected to move on to something else someday, he still didn't feel he'd accomplished all he wanted to at SHS. Now the decision to stay or move on had been taken away from him. And to make matters worse, the building to which he'd been assigned next year was run by a man with whom Hiles had a "profoundly deep personality conflict." So Hiles was in the awkward situation of having enough seniority to guarantee himself a teaching job in the district, but no way to secure a head-coaching position in track, because coaching choices rested solely with the building principals.

Hiles had no idea what he was going to do. He was a competent and enthusiastic teacher but his real love was coaching. And he was excellent at that. Three times he'd been named State Track Coach of the Year. He had guided his teams to the state championship seven times, a record that many felt would go unbroken for years and years, perhaps forever. He'd been invited to national coaching conventions to lecture on training methods in his specialty, middle- and long-distance running. In everyone's mind but his own, he'd done it all. Hiles believed there was still plenty to do.

Marty reached for the bottom drawer of the first cabinet and began his transfer ritual. Hiles had given him very specific instructions. First, he was to make sure the folders weren't fattened by duplicates. "No use crippling ourselves by carrying more than we have to, right?" said Hiles. Second, Marty was to make sure nothing in the folders was misfiled. Finally, he was to place them in the yearbook boxes in the proper chronological order, "not haphazardly, as if nothing mattered but getting done." It was not a cushy job. Marty had already worked a week on the files and he wasn't even done with the first of the dull-gray, four-drawer steel cabinets. He knew that sooner or later he'd be working overtime.

He had pulled the bottom drawer open and lifted out a

batch of five folders and was about to go through them at Coach Hiles's desk when the east wall of the office diverted his attention. There hung the pictures of all those past athletes who for one reason or another had been named SUPER SALUKIS and inducted into HILES'S HALL OF FAME (as the stenciled sign over the display proclaimed). Marty wandered closer to the collection, one he had perused often in the past but which continued to fascinate him. He looked at the faces, recalled how he'd learned things about them. Sometimes Coach Hiles had reminisced in front of him. Other times the older brother or sister of one of Marty's friends had told him anecdotes about these stars.

Marty's eyes roamed from picture to picture, row to row, year to year, event to event. There were sprinters, milers, discus throwers, shot-putters, high jumpers, pole-vaulters, hurdlers. There were only boys throughout the early years of Hiles's reign, and then a smattering of girl champions appeared later on. Among the girls he found her. Stacy Davis. Marty stepped closer to her picture, one he'd studied carefully before. He took a deep breath.

She was photographed standing on the victory steps at the region meet. She was only a sophomore then. Her tall, slim, tightly muscled and beautifully proportioned body was erect. Around her neck hung the medal she'd just won. Her curly dark hair looked freshly styled, and she was smiling confidently right into the camera, her big brown eager and innocent eyes squinting from her grin. Marty was momentarily startled by the resemblance Stacy bore here to his lost summer love, Debi Donnovan. He realized that was what attracted him to Debi, the facial similarity. He shook his head, amused, but he also felt a faint clogging at

---

the back of his throat—desire. "Do I know you?" he asked softly.

He bent to read the three-by-five card under Stacy's picture. On it Hiles had typed: "Racey-Stacy Davis, Southwestern's First Female Regional Champion, Two-Mile Run." Her winning time was listed. Next to that was an asterisk and the word *RECORD!*

Suddenly, Marty felt angry. He'd always hoped to join this elite group. But now, even if his performance at the state meet justified his being inducted, it would be for nothing, because the Hall of Fame was scheduled to come down like everything else at SHS when the building closed.

"C'mon, get to work, huh?" said Coach Hiles from the doorway, surprising Marty so much that he flinched and spun around. Hiles was smiling, holding his clipboard; his silver whistle was hanging on a leather cord around his neck. His high forehead was wrinkled by the smile that showed his straight white teeth. He was still in great shape. He could still run a little himself. He even made his phys. ed. garb look good, gave a certain dignity to the maroon polyester slacks and gold knit shirt. "Want to see your schedule for the week before you get back to business?" He was pointing to the file cabinets with his clipboard.

"Sure."

Hiles handed Marty a typed sheet summarizing his workouts. Marty nodded as he scanned it. "Guess I'll be busy. It looks tougher than I expected."

"It is tougher. It's the last roundup, and you're going to be ready. We won't start pointing until next week."

Marty glanced off, nodded again. At least there was relief in sight: "pointing" meant doing light workouts the two days prior to a meet, in this case the state meet. Hiles followed Marty's stare to what was distracting him.

"You like her?" Hiles asked. "The mystery girl?"

Marty brought his gaze back to Hiles and searched for something clever to say. He came up empty.

"Stacy Davis," said Hiles.

"I know."

"You read the card."

"I knew her when I was little."

"Yeah?"

"She was my baby-sitter."

"She was?"

"I mean the night she, you know, disappeared."

"What?! You serious?"

"I was the kid. I was there, up in my room."

Hiles stared at Marty. His arms dropped to his sides, his lips parted slightly. "I don't believe it," he mumbled. "Why didn't you ever mention that? Why didn't your dad? We've known each other a long time."

"I don't know," Marty said.

Marty did know that when he was in junior high school, his father had done a detailed article on Coach Hiles and his program and his stars—present and past—one of whom had placed in the Pan Am games. Long before the interview, John Hiles and Ken Oliver had been track rivals themselves. Their high school teams competed against one another half a dozen times, but the two athletes never met in a head-to-head contest. Hiles was an outstanding distance runner while Ken Oliver was a high jumper.

"This is really something," Hiles said. He looked at the picture for a few moments, then commented, "Old Stacy. She was the first real 'Goodie' in the girls' program."

Marty smiled at the peculiar label his coach substituted for "superstar" whenever he referred to his champion distance runners.

"What I mean is," continued Hiles, "she was so far ahead of her time. She was the first girl I ever coached who could get outside of herself every practice, every race. She could run and run and never be conscious of herself as an individual who was suffering punishment. But you understand all that." Before Marty could comment, Hiles added, "I mean, she still holds records . . . *still!*"

Marty watched Hiles as he nodded, apparently acknowledging the documented greatness of Stacy Davis. "But then . . ."

"Yeah," said Marty. "Then."

"It must have been a terrible ordeal for you."

"It was bad," Marty replied.

"Where were you when it happened? In bed asleep?"

"Under my bed asleep. I guess the noise must've scared me, made me hide."

"It's a good thing."

"I don't know," Marty said, staring at the floor.

"Of course it was. What could you have done that was any smarter?"

"There must have been something."

"No way. Don't hang that on yourself. Forget it."

Marty shrugged, smiled.

"What's funny?"

"That's what my mother always says. 'Forget it.'"

"That's a dumb thing to say, huh. I don't suppose you'll ever forget it."

"Not parts of it, anyway."

"Like what?"

"I heard something I still don't understand."

"You heard her?"

"She screamed but she wasn't just yelling. She was call-

34

ing to me, I know it. My dad's even got an old tape record-ing of me telling the story the day after it happened. I used to listen to it, but it didn't help. Things never got any clearer. They still haven't."

Hiles nodded, gazed once again at the color photo of Stacy Davis. "She was something. She was the girl. Did you know her very well?"

"I like to think so."

"In many ways she was very typical, very predictable," Hiles said, his voice soft. "But as the year ended she began changing. She seemed different. She started having all kinds of problems with authority."

Marty looked questioningly at his coach.

"I mean, she had spirit and pride, everything it takes, you know? But then she started to show a kind of daredevil courage. Suddenly, she wanted to test the limits of every-thing, including my patience. She wanted to push herself past the limits.

"In practice she sometimes worked so hard she scared me. She was getting self-destructive. After a while I began to feel I just wasn't in touch with her anymore, that she didn't want my help anymore. Despite all that, the point is she was the first Goodie in her particular program." Hiles paused for effect, then asked, "You know what that makes you, in your program?"

"No," said Marty, genuinely mystified as he contem-plated a Stacy Davis who had never seemed "different" to him.

"Marty, I don't want this to sound corny, but you've got a better than good chance to make a super showing in the state mile this year. You know that."

Marty nodded.

"And with the school closing and the cutbacks and the declining enrollment districtwide, well isn't it obvious?"

Marty shrugged, looked confused.

"You could be the last one I have."

"The last what? The Last Goodie?"

"Absolutely."

"Oh, I don't think so, Coach," Marty said quickly. "They won't keep you off the track for very long." Marty was pleased to give his coach some encouragement for a change. The man had already given him so much, helped him so much.

Hiles, lost in thought, stared at the space over Marty's right shoulder. Suddenly he jerked up his forearm and looked at his watch. "Geez, I gotta run. You know this class is full of skulls. By now they've probably maimed somebody over a disputed point. You keep at those files. And please be careful. I don't care how long it takes you. Just so it's done right."

"Okay," Marty said, smiling at Hiles's extravagant use of his T.A.'s time.

Hiles rushed out of the office, closed the door behind him, leaving Marty alone with the folders.

Marty had worked his way through three-fourths of the bottom drawer of the first cabinet when he found it: an unopened letter addressed simply to "Coach Hiles." A girl's handwriting. The letter was loose, stuck behind the file containing the girls' state-meet results of twelve years ago, not a championship year for the ladies. Marty placed the letter on the coach's desk and continued packing the folders. He'd finished the top drawer of the second cabinet when the bell ending the period rang, freeing him.

Heaving a sigh of relief, he left the office and headed for

his gym locker, anxious as always to suit up for practice. He would train hard this week. He would do all his coach asked of him. He would do more than that even. He would do whatever he had to do to win. He would be the Last Goodie. Why not?

Just as Marty was about to leave the locker room and join his teammates in the sunny warmth of another beautiful May afternoon, Ted Harper cornered him. Marty was stunned. Harper was serious, frowning, troubled, so unlike his usual self. Marty guessed they'd finally connected him with the Parker Olympiad Moonshot and that Harper had been suspended again, at the worst possible time.

Marty asked, "What's wrong?"

"I'm sick of it, that's what. I've had it."

"With what?"

"All this 'Shadow Man' bull. That's all over now, understand?" Harper looked Marty straight in the eye, his typically bright face a study in stony resolve.

"Gimme the punch line," said Marty, convinced that this had to be some kind of put-on.

"It's no joke, chump. I'm sick of being criticized for not producing more, for not whippin' you once in a while. Some of these local newspapers are making me into a psycho case almost."

"C'mon, Teddy, I don't—"

"I'm not through," Harper cut in. His tone was so uncharacteristically mean that Marty was taken aback. He didn't think Harper was trying to intimidate him exactly, or threaten him. He was trying to say something important, straight for a change. "Listen to me, okay?"

Marty said, "I'm listening."

"I just want to tell you that from now on, till the end of

the season, if you beat me, it's because you really beat me, not because I'm screwin' off or something. Not because I 'lack the will to win' or because I'm 'not concentrating at the finish line' or whatever the hell else they say about me. From now on, in practice, in regions, wherever, the race won't be over till . . . it's over!" He paused, thought about what he'd just said, broke into a big self-mocking smile and added, "Original line, huh?" Then he turned away and was out the locker-room door before Marty could reply.

And after practice Marty still didn't know what to think, because for the first time ever, for the first time in three years of practices and meets, Ted Harper beat Marty in a "challenge race," beat him badly, buried him with a finishing kick that left Marty in second place by five yards.

"Ain't nothin' lasts forever," Harper had said to him when it was over, with a smile that said the challenge had just begun.

CHAPTER
FIVE

"It's okay, honey. Really. Relax now."
 Muffled crying, a pause . . .
"What's wrong? What was it?"
"He's coming back?" a weak, gasping little-boy voice replied.
"No. No, he's not coming back. I won't let him." His father talking, soothing him. A pause. "You were dreaming. Did you see anything?"
"Stacy is yelling."
"Can you hear?"
"What?"
"Did you hear what she said?"
Another pause.
"Marty?"
"Huh?" A troubled sigh.
"What did she say?"
"You know."
"Tell me again. Can you tell me again?"

"It was the same. 'NO! . . . GEE! . . . SKURD!'—like that."

"'NO—GEE—SKURD,'" his father repeated quietly, as though he were contemplating it.

"Yes."

"You're sure."

"What?" Followed by an audible yawn.

"Nothing, honey. It's okay. Go back to sleep."

"Where's Peter Pelican?"

"Here. He fell out of bed, but he never goes very far. He's always here, with you."

"Oh."

"You hug up Peter, okay? I'm right here, too."

"Can you stay in my room, Daddy? You could go camping on the floor like last time."

"Sure. You go back to sleep now. I'll be camping down here."

"Okay . . . g'night."

Two clicks, a stop and a start, and then his father's voice whispering the date and time of the recording.

The tape had been made at approximately 2:00 A.M. on a Monday, just a month after the taking of Stacy Davis. As Marty popped the cassette from his player and glanced at his watch, he saw that ironically his circumstances hadn't changed much. Once again he'd been denied sleep by an emotional upset, a literal upset, only this one shouldn't have been nearly as unnerving as his adventure in terror twelve years ago. Tonight, though, he hadn't slept at all, and now it was 1:00 A.M., Tuesday, only the beginning of a long school week.

The shock had kept him awake, the shock and his own

embarrassed disbelief, his suddenly clear awareness of just how fragile a concept like self-confidence can be. He'd been completely unable to explain Harper's victory to himself, how he'd let the race get away that afternoon. Marty thought he'd been concentrating, pacing himself correctly, pushing himself appropriately at the end. But Harper . . . Harper flew by him so fast down the stretch it seemed as though Ted had just come sprinting onto the track, that he hadn't actually run the previous, grueling three and a half laps.

Because he wasn't sleeping, Marty had decided to listen to some of the old tapes. It wasn't something he'd felt like doing the last few years, but with his mother gone he could at least do it openly now. She couldn't harp on him to just forget it all.

As he put that early tape back into its plastic case, he remembered something, became suddenly puzzled by something, a discrepancy. He walked over to his desk, opened one of the two big side drawers, and dug out his essay, his narrative/experience, the paper he'd reread just last Saturday. And sure enough, there it was.

"NO! . . . TSEE! . . . HURT!!"—phrasing that suddenly seemed far different from what he'd heard himself saying on the tape: "NO! . . . GEE! . . . SKURD!"

Yawning finally, Marty put the essay on the desk top, leaving it out to remind himself that tomorrow he'd mention the inconsistency to his father. As for now, listening and thinking had made him tired, just as worrying had kept him awake. He got up from the desk chair, turned off the reading light, and crawled back into bed. For several minutes he stared at the ceiling and wondered where his mother was, what country or city, why she wasn't around when he needed her. Maybe she was right. Maybe forgetting would be best.

Soon his thoughts drifted to recollections of terrible things that had happened to other fine, seasoned milers on their way to the state meet. Just last year, there was a boy from The Iron Range named Carstens who'd run decent qualifying times almost all year, but who had a horrible day at his regional and never even appeared in the state finals. Others, a few from past teams at Southwestern, dropped out because of nagging little injuries. Some were mentally flat during the championship heat. Even though they'd looked good during the regions and prelims, when faced with the final four laps their intensity evaporated like infield dew at ten in the morning, and they faded to no-shows down the stretch.

Seconds before Marty slid mercifully off to sleep, he looked inside, searched deep into his own heart to see if it was still there: the desire, the fanatical will to win it all, at all costs. He was still looking when he fell asleep.

The next day at practice Marty was exhausted before the team began warm-ups. When he found Harper staring at him, donning a little smile of superiority that reminded Marty of yesterday's failings, Marty had no idea how to react. He chose to say nothing, make no comment that could be misinterpreted. Ted was his friend. Instead, Marty finished calisthenics hoping for divine intervention, a miracle, because he knew after he'd completed his workout, his timed runs and dashes, his "jogging rests," his weight training, Coach Hiles would expect him eagerly to challenge Harper for the number-one miler spot. He'd be expected to win it back. Marty wasn't sure he could even complete a challenge race, he felt so tired.

Suddenly, there he was, right next to him, talking to him in low tones—Hiles. Marty got up from his leg stretches and said, "What?"

"That letter on my desk yesterday—did you put it there?"

Marty was confused. Coach Hiles seemed to be trying to talk softly while all around them guys clapped, chanted, and wisecracked as the warm-up drills were counted out by an assistant coach.

Marty said, "Yeah, I found it in the files."

"Which one?"

"Just behind the state-meet results from I think twelve years ago, both boys' and girls'. You didn't exactly dominate that year," Marty added, smiling.

Normally Hiles would have reacted to Marty's small effort at sarcasm with some witty rebuke, but today he ignored the comment completely.

"You read it?" he asked cautiously, quietly.

Marty looked up and found himself eye to eye with his mentor. "Coach, it was sealed. I didn't steam it open then glue it back shut or something—no."

Hiles looked away, barely nodding, staring vacantly at one of the team's managers as he readied the high-jump pit for practice. "Okay," Hiles said at last. "Get good and loose. Have a strong practice. Look sharp today in your challenge race. It's too late now to . . ."

Marty stood waiting for the rest of Hiles's sentence.

"What, Coach?"

"Too late for you to . . . lose your concentration. You're beyond that. Put yesterday behind you."

Marty's eyes were downcast. He realized the Pressure was on him, full blast. But Hiles's pep talk just now seemed prefabricated, as if he were mouthing the words and thinking about something else entirely.

Throughout the first half of practice Marty felt horrible. He was so fatigued and groggy from his nearly sleepless night, day of demanding classes, and afternoon of drills that by the time he lined up with Harper for the challenge race he was already leg heavy, already struggling. Marty knew it would take an extraordinary effort to beat Harper today. Ted seemed suddenly possessed.

At the starting line Marty leaned forward, arms hanging, wrists loose. He inhaled a last deep breath and watched Hiles raise the little nickel-plated pistol above his head. Finally, the crack of the gun shattered the tense silence and both runners shot down the track, rounded the first turn matching strides, Marty running on the outside. Coming off the turn, Marty glanced sidelong at Harper and found him unsmiling, staring straight ahead, a knot of muscle showing along his clenched jaws, his eyes grim with determination.

Marty knew the pace was fast, too fast, faster than he himself would have chosen if he'd been feeling great instead of god-awful. When they reached the end of the backstretch of their first lap, Harper's strategy was plain. Ted wanted to run Marty off the track, intimidate him permanently. For a change, Harper was holding nothing back. His taste of victory yesterday had made him hungry for another heaping portion.

At the end of lap one Marty was still at Harper's shoulder. Hiles was hollering encouragement as he looked at his stopwatch; his maroon baseball cap, with the gold letters S H S stenciled across the front, was sitting back on his head. "Keep 'er goin'!" he yelled. "Let's see what you got! Keep 'er goin'!"

Halfway through the second quarter mile Marty realized the only way to deal with Harper was to best him at his own game, to up the ante, to open the burners and kill him with speed and pace. Marty did that sometimes to obnoxious opponents. He was used to relying on something extra that other guys didn't have or, more accurately, never used: a small reserve of energy that gave him the acceleration he needed when he needed it. But he was used to drawing from this last-resort source during the final sprint to the finish line, when every step had consequence. Now, however, he was only halfway into his second lap.

Running on his toes, his pin spikes tapping a rapid staccato on the springy asphalt, his lungs already seared from stress, ready to surrender to exhaustion, Marty called up his reserve and began stretching out. He pulled one, then two, then three strides ahead of Harper, so that when they passed Hiles the second time, Marty was in his customary position. All Marty wanted to do now was hold off Harper, just . . . stay . . . ahead.

Marty maintained his lead through most of the third lap, his chest heaving, aching, his legs starting to numb and knot, his stomach cramping, sending spasms up and down and back and forth across his torso. He ran as close to the inside curve of the track as he dared. He wanted to be sure he was running the shortest distance necessary to win the race. He knew that each foot out from the curb added an extra three feet around one turn. As he threw himself forward along the last turn of lap three, he heard Harper coming up on him, heard teammates who'd stopped practicing to watch the race yelling and cheering.

Marty attempted to lengthen his stride just another few

---

inches, just enough to keep Harper from pulling even and passing, enough to keep him to the outside and running a longer race. But when Marty made the mistake of looking back for Harper, the unthinkable happened. He took his eyes off the curve in front of him, and the edge of his left foot caught the concrete rim lining the inside of the track. He lost his balance and slammed down hard against the gritty surface, rolling, sliding, scraping his palms, one elbow, a knee, and a shoulder. As he did so, Harper rushed past him and disappeared around the turn.

Marty made a gutsy effort to get up and continue the chase, but his legs had turned to rubber. He made three faltering strides and then stumbled to the infield, where he collapsed. To him the fall was not terrible—it was horrible. He was angry about losing, but frightened by how he'd lost. For this race had proved to be the real-life enactment of another of his most provocative nightmares.

Not so long ago, Jim Ryun had the same thing happen to him. Ryun, the greatest middle- and long-distance runner of his time and one of Marty's few athlete heroes, was America's first high school runner to do a sub-four-minute mile in high school competition. But Marty had also read about Ryun's disastrous spill at the Olympics in Munich. He was racing in a preliminary heat where he had only to place fourth to survive and advance. However, while he was threading his way through the pack near the end of the race, Ryun tripped on Vitus Ashaba's heel and stumbled into Billy Fordjour of Ghana. Both Ryun and Fordjour fell and dropped from the race. Ryun came home a loser, returning to America so depressed and humiliated that supposedly he once considered suicide. He had dedicated his talents and time to achieving one special goal, and when he failed three times to obtain it he couldn't make peace with himself. It was an experience Marty Oliver could never get out of his mind.

So nearly every time he ran in an important race, which now meant every race, Marty would sprint to the lead and hold on to it more from a fear of being tripped than because of some unbridled exuberance or superiority complex. And until now that approach had been wholly successful. But today, at last, at a bad time, another nightmare had come true.

Light-headed, hurting, Marty tried again to get to his feet. As he did, Harper ran by and called, "You okay?"

Marty stood up straight and waved at Harper just moments before he heard a rushing wind behind his head, saw a swirling blackness above his eyes, and toppled back into a fall that threatened never to end. The next thing Marty remembered was being walked from the field, a teammate supporting him under each arm, Hiles muttering something about the emergency room and fluid loss and calling Marty's father.

By the time they got him to the locker room, Marty knew he wouldn't need hospitalization. What he needed was rest, some salve, a few bandages, and more rest. He needed time to relax, to reorganize, to adjust to the fact that, for whatever reason, Ted Harper had just defeated him in two straight mile runs. Two straight. At that point, Marty decided it was okay to panic.

CHAPTER
SIX

Wednesday, Marty stayed home. He slept in, nursed his wounded arms and legs, nursed his wounded ego. He had just awakened, looked at his digital alarm clock, and discovered it was already 9:15. He didn't know his dad's schedule because it changed nearly every day. He stretched, thought about his father's job. He envied him his career. It seemed to have more pluses than minuses. For example, all the negative pressures like having to meet deadlines, deal with screwy editors, and persuade closed-minded publishers—those difficulties were more than off-set by the freedom to move about, the flexible hours, the diversity of assignments.

Marty pushed off the covers and looked at his aching, bandaged wounds. He was lucky in one sense. He hadn't done any muscle, tendon, or ligament damage in his fall from grace. "It's only a flesh wound," his dad had said. That was last night. The doctor had also told him he needed rest, that he was dehydrated and exhausted.

It wasn't difficult, then, to let school slide for a day. Ken

Oliver believed in keeping schedules, but as always (where his son was concerned) rationality prevailed over principle.

With his feet on the floor, Marty was about to test his tender limbs by walking to the bathroom. He was moving stiffly through the upstairs hallway when the phone rang. He counted two rings as he hobbled into his parents' bedroom and grabbed for the extension on the nightstand next to their bed. He'd taken a quick breath and was about to say hello when his father picked up the phone downstairs and beat him to it.

"Oliver's," said his dad.

Marty listened to make sure the call wasn't for him.

"Ken?" the caller said, his voice familiar.

"Yes."

"John Hiles here, Ken. How're you?"

"Hey! Hello-hello. I'm fine. What's new? What's up?"

Marty smiled at the warm and enthusiastic tone of his father's voice. He knew his dad liked and respected the coach.

"I'm calling to ask about that clumsy kid of yours."

"I think he's still sleeping, John. He was more tired than hurt yesterday. I'm afraid he's worried about the state meet. He hasn't been able to relax lately."

"Ken, I think he's worried about Harper."

"Harper? Ted Harper?"

"Sure. Didn't he tell you?"

"Tell me what?"

Marty felt uncomfortable, childish, eavesdropping on his own father. It made him seem small and sneaky and cheap. But now he was destined to listen to the whole conversation, because if he tried to hang up in mid-dialogue he'd be heard and detected anyway.

"Didn't he tell you Harper beat him out?"

"He what?"

"Harper challenged him on Monday and won. And yesterday during the rematch Marty fell, so Harper won again . . . by default."

"No. No, he didn't mention it. But I should've known something important had happened. I think he was up very late Monday night."

"Thinking too much about Harper, probably."

"Maybe."

Hiles waited a moment before saying, "I've got another problem, Ken. Something else that concerns you, and Marty."

Marty's wandering attention refocused abruptly, riveting itself again on the conversation. He tried to anticipate the revelation.

"And what's that?"

"I don't suppose Marty mentioned the letter either."

"Not at all. What letter? John, this conversation sounds like dialogue from Midnight Mystery."

Hiles laughed. "No mention of the letter, huh?"

"None. Zilch. I think what we have here is a failure to communicate."

"It's just as well. Anyway, while Marty was going through the files, cleaning them up and repacking them, he found a sealed letter. . . ."

"And?"

"It was written and put in the drawer twelve years ago. Twelve. It's from a girl named Lisa Walker. Ring a bell?"

"Nope."

"Lisa Walker was a so-so hurdler on one of our first girls' teams. But more important, she was once Stacy Davis's best friend."

"What's in the letter, John?" asked Ken Oliver, his voice deadly serious now. "Do I dare ask?"

"We better talk about this in person, in private. I shouldn't go into it on the phone. Will you be home later tonight?"

"Let's see . . . what does 'later' mean?"

Marty heard his father rustling some papers. He was undoubtedly sitting at his desk, shoving manuscript pages around, looking for his appointment book. The little calendar pamphlet was usually left on top of the debris but always disappeared whenever he really needed it.

"John, it looks all clear after ten. That too late?"

"Not for this."

"You want to come over here?"

"If it's okay. Will Marty still be up?"

"Probably."

"Good. I should talk to him too. We need to get him thinking more about running and fun and less about fear and losing. He'll win because he's prepared himself. He should know that, but kids . . ."

"I understand."

"Worrying won't beat anybody."

"No, it won't."

"See you around ten."

"I'll be watching. You remember how to get over here?"

"No problem."

Marty tried to hang up with his father. He wanted no telltale clicks revealing his shabby behavior. By the time he placed the receiver over the already depressed button, Marty felt sure he'd pulled it off. He slipped back into the hallway and headed for the bathroom.

When he was finished there, his face washed and hair

combed, he stepped out and walked right into his father. Marty gave a little gasp of surprise, smiled nervously.

His father smiled back and asked, "Why didn't you tell me about Harper?"

Marty thought for a second. He knew he had to respond without revealing his eavesdropping. "Harper?" he asked back.

"Ted Harper. He beat you out. Remember now?"

"I fell. I told you that," Marty replied, warming to his role, wondering how far he should push it.

"Look, don't play games with me. Who do you think you're dealing with here? That was Hiles on the phone, and he said that on Monday Harper—"

"Okay, okay," Marty broke in quickly, feeling confident now that he'd gotten away cleanly. "I guess I wasn't concentrating. But even though I felt like checking out on Tuesday, I still raced him and was up on him pretty good when I tripped myself. I could've won, I think. I don't know."

"So why didn't you tell me about Monday?"

"I didn't see you."

Marty's father heaved a sigh and shook his head. "Whatever," he concluded. "Well look, you take it easy today. Relax, sleep if you can. Coach Hiles wants to talk to you later. He's coming over tonight."

"Yeah? Over here?"

"Exactly." His father smiled.

"Okay."

"Will you be all right?"

"Fine. I'll manage."

Before leaving to "talk to some people," Ken Oliver made certain Marty had something in the refrigerator worth eating. As Marty watched him go, he felt proud. He was proud of the way his dad looked, the way he dressed, the way he wrote, the way they got along.

Alone for the rest of the morning and most of the afternoon, Marty decided, after a quick bowl of cereal, to continue reviewing the taped conversations he'd made with his father following the Stacy dreams. He went to the box and pulled out a cassette dated five years ago. Marty snapped it into his tape player and winced visibly as his puberty-stricken, cracking junior-high voice was broadcast around the room.

"Marty?"

"Huh?"

"Can you tell me about it? Can you remember anything? It's important."

"I know."

A long pause . . . his breathing, audible at first, coming in raspy staggering breaths, eventually evened. Then:

"Outside . . ."

"What's outside?"

"I was walking . . . at night. And I'm walking all alone, and pretty soon this car, like a sports car, long and low . . . this car comes up to me and slows way down and kind of coasts, and the guy revs up the engine as it coasts along beside me and moves right with me. When I stop, it stops too and so I looked to see who's driving it. . . ."

"And? You see anybody, someone you recognized?"

"All I could see was his arm. He was calling me over to the car, you know, like this . . ."

"Waving you over."

"Yeah."

"Then what?"

"I ran. I ran and ran and the whole time this guy stayed right with me, pumping the engine, you know, racing it. I kept running . . . and that was it."

"You woke up?"

"Yeah, I guess so. I don't remember anymore."

"Did you hear a car sound like that after Stacy screamed?"

A brief silence.

"No. I think it was before."

"Before? Before what?"

"Earlier. Before I even went to bed. We were in the living room and we were playing hide-and-seek and I was behind the couch, you know, when it was by the front window? Remember?"

"Sure. Then what?"

"Well, I was hiding there and that's when I think I heard it . . . out front. The engine sounds, I mean."

"Just once?"

"Maybe. I was hiding for a long time before Stacy found me."

Silence for a good fifteen seconds. Then:

"You know what I just remembered?"

"Unh-uh."

"She even climbed on the couch to look out the front window, and I was right under her nose and she didn't see me."

"Did you look outside too?"

"I think so."

"Did you look when you heard the noise?"

"I suppose. I can't remember exactly."

"You see anything, a car you might remember now?"

"I don't know. It's not very clear anymore. It was dark and I was hiding and that's when Stacy caught me."

"When you were looking out the window."

"Yeah. She scared me, real bad. She grabbed me from the back and said, 'BOO!!' and I almost jumped through the window. I banged against it. We scared each other I think."

"Did Stacy say anything about a car outside?"

"I don't remember."

"Did she ask what you were looking at outside?"

"I don't think so."

Another fifteen second pause.

"You all right now? Can you go back to sleep?"

"I guess so. Dad?"

"What?"

"Nothing . . . just, well, you know . . . thanks."

"Marty, you didn't wake Mom. Don't mention this to her, okay?"

"I know."

Machine clicks marked the end of the recording session and Marty was left where he started, in darkness. Anxious and nervous, he got up and did something else he hadn't done in years. He walked out of his room and followed the reconstructed, the assumed movements Stacy had made that night.

He descended the stairs, passed through the living room, where she'd been doing her homework, turned into the dining area, and headed for the kitchen. Marty knew Stacy probably wouldn't recognize the place now, the redecorating had been that extensive. Marty thought his par-

---

ents had been trying to change houses without actually moving. When he entered the kitchen and began slowly approaching the door to the basement steps, his throat felt dry. Once in the basement, he stared down the long, lavishly finished rec room at the one detail that served as a constant reminder of the Incident.

At the far end of the basement was the three-by-five-foot window Marty's father had had installed when Marty was little. He'd put it in for air circulation. Marty's play area had been down there. Now the window was secured with three different kinds of locks. Outside, his father had hung a steel-mesh screen that was screwed to the window frame with 3-inch lag bolts. The window and the walkout door, which had also been given additional locks, hadn't been opened since Stacy's disappearance. Now no one could get in. Still, Marty didn't like coming down here. He was never completely comfortable in the house alone. He took one more long look around, expelled a deep breath, and ascended the stairs.

They were there, he realized—all those old feelings.

CHAPTER

SEVEN

After lunch Marty slept, slept deeply and dreamlessly.
Later in the afternoon he went out and sat in a chaise
longue on the patio. He wore only running shorts and
thongs. He wanted to get some sun and relax a little longer.
He'd brought out a book to read, but in spite of the ideal
weather—warm, clear, windless, soothing—the next hour
brought on another attack of nervous anxiety. Marty wasn't
sure what was bothering him. The prospect of facing Coach
Hiles? The possibility of learning the contents of the Mystery Letter? The fact that he was still the number-two
miler at Southwestern?

Following an uneventful supper, Marty went to his room to
catch up on his math and wait for his coach. It was, as
scheduled, a little past ten o'clock when Hiles rang the
doorbell. He was welcomed by Marty's father, who'd come
home some time before. Marty got up, walked quietly over
to his bedroom door, opened it, stepped silently into the

hall, and tiptoed to the top of the stairs. He was on his second eavesdropping mission of the day.

"Remember the last time we did this, Ken?"

"Could I forget? I never got so much mail."

Marty knew they were referring to the long personality profile his dad had done about four years ago on Coach Hiles.

Marty heard them moving toward his father's office. "So, what's this about a letter?" Ken Oliver asked.

"I should probably talk with the kid first," said Hiles. "Is he still up?"

"I'll see."

Marty backpedaled quickly and quietly to his room. He slid inside and eased the door shut and had just returned to his desk when his father called out, "Marty?"

"Yeah, Dad," he hollered back.

"C'mon down here. Your mentor has arrived."

"Huh? . . . What?"

"Your *coach* is here. Hustle down!"

Marty smiled to himself and headed for the stairs.

"How're you feeling?" Hiles asked when Marty appeared before him in the living room. Both his father and Hiles were standing.

"Better. I slept a lot today."

"What about the leg burns? You keep them clean and covered?"

"Yup."

"Good. That's good."

For a few seconds the three of them—father, son, and coach—stood grinning awkwardly at one another. Marty was about to attempt a graceful exit when Hiles spoke up.

"Listen," he began, "we should talk about regions, okay?"

"Sure," said Marty with a nervous half smile.

"Here's my theory, but if you don't like it, you'll be free to make your own suggestions."

Marty nodded and looked at the floor.

"What I think you should do is just relax until Saturday. Take light workouts tomorrow and Friday, start pointing now, and enter the regions as the second miler. It'll make a difference at the starting line, sure. But not that much of one. We want to avoid disaster, right? Some totally unnecessary catastrophe, the kind of thing that happened yesterday. That could've done it, you know? It's frightening. So, how about it? Can you live with that approach . . . ?" Hiles made a rolling gesture with his hand.

"What?" said Marty.

"Can you accept that role . . . psychologically? Can you handle it?"

Marty stared at Hiles. "What's with Harper?" he asked. "Did you scare him or something? Is he on some experimental drug?" Marty was smiling.

"Nope. Absolutely not. On both counts. I don't know where Teddy got his new devotion to running and winning. I just don't know. But I'll tell you, from my point of view anyway, it's kind of fun to see. I'm glad for him. And I'm glad about what he's doing for you. I know you'll rise to the challenge. It could be a very healthy situation for the team. You agree?"

"It'll be a two-man race after half a lap anyway, right? Isn't that what you're figuring?"

"That's what I'd planned, but . . ."

"But?"

"There's something else you should know. They've sort

---

of stacked our region. They've included at least two other quality kids you haven't faced yet, both from private schools."

"No lie."

"Unh-uh. So, what'll it be?"

"You're the coach. I let myself fall into this, so I guess I have to work my way out. Whatever you say is all right."

"Good. Well that's about all I had. I'll set you up with a lighter workout tomorrow."

"Okay," said Marty as he left the room. "See ya."

"Good night, Marty," said his father and Hiles in unison. The three of them shared a laugh. "We could audition as a Greek chorus, Coach," said Ken Oliver.

Marty climbed the stairs, walked to his room, opened and closed the door without going in, and tiptoed back to the top of the stairs. Now he felt like a kid trying to spy on Santa. His heart sank when he heard his father say, "We'd better talk about this in my office."

As Hiles and Ken Oliver walked through the living room en route to the office, Marty had to decide his next move. He wanted to know about the letter. He wasn't exactly sure why. It was just that recently, for the last couple of weeks anyway, everything had started to seem related, as if the past and the present weren't separate anymore, as if his whole life were happening at once. He couldn't explain the feeling any better than that.

So when Marty heard the office door close, he made his choice. He decided to risk eavesdropping still another time. He was in it now anyway, all the way. He'd already overheard enough, maybe too much. He couldn't ignore what he knew. Besides, he was the one who'd found the letter. And by now he'd gained considerable confidence in his skill as a covert operator. He'd had nothing but success thus far. He started down the stairs.

By the time he'd worked his way to the office door, the discussion on the other side had become intense, lively.

"And this . . . this Lisa Walker," his father was asking, "never made any other attempt to contact you, to talk to you about the problem?"

"No. None. Like I said, she ran hurdles for me. She was on the squad with Stacy, but we weren't close. She was very shy. We talked track when we talked at all. She was a nice kid, though. Reliable. I remember that much. Not real cute, nowhere near as talented as Stacy, of course, but then who was. And I think Lisa was a year older than Stacy."

"This is unbelievable. . . ."

"I agree."

"Where is she now? Have any idea?"

"Lisa? I haven't the slightest."

"Well. As I see it, we've got to do at least two things right away. Somehow we've got to get over to Davis's old place and see if the journal is still there. I'll have to call Eldon in on this."

"Who?"

"Eldon Taggert. A cop friend. Homicide detective. Geez, I wonder how many times that home has been bought and sold since the Davises left. Or remodeled."

"What was the other thing we had to do?" Hiles asked.

"Find Lisa Walker, of course. Talk to her, jog her memory. I hope she's still available, somewhere."

"It's all such a long shot," commented Hiles.

"At the risk of sounding trite, it's our only shot. The only one we've had in years."

"I'm still amazed that we never talked about this before.

I'm not surprised very often, but your kid got to me the other day."

"He tell you everything?"

"Pretty much."

"The dreams?"

"A little bit."

"We've been fighting it all the time, trying to bury it. His mother always felt it was best to let it drop. But Marty's dreams didn't go away. So it floats up every now and then, all by itself. Obviously, this letter changes everything."

"Yes, it does."

"Can I hang on to it until tomorrow? I'll get some copies made, one for very safekeeping, and one for you."

"Don't bother. I already made a copy. This is a hot item."

After a short pause, Ken Oliver asked, "Anything else we need to think about?"

"Only how much I appreciate your willingness to help. This isn't going to be easy, for anybody."

"But there's something in it for everybody. I'm glad you brought it to me. We just might have our break."

"The journal?"

"Uh-huh."

A long silence passed before Marty's father said, "I'll keep this in a safe place."

Marty didn't wait for Hiles's reply. He knew the conversation was over, that they'd soon be leaving the office. He scuttled through the house and back up the stairs. From inside his bedroom he listened while Hiles and his father said their farewells in the front hallway. For the next few hours Marty forced himself to stay awake. Finally, when the house was hauntingly silent and dark, Marty ventured forth once more, going quietly downstairs to his father's office.

With him he carried a flashlight that he didn't use until he was safe inside the office, with the door closed behind him. When he clicked the flashlight on, he began searching, playing the percentages, looking first where his father usually put papers he hadn't felt like filing. Marty smiled as he lifted the blotter on the wide oak desk and found the little pink envelope he'd discovered just two days before. He eased the letter out, thinking how rapidly things had changed for him since Monday.

The letter was twelve years old, dated May 27, almost eight months after Stacy disappeared. It was written in ballpoint pen, blue, on looseleaf paper that had been torn out of a spiral notebook; the ragged edges of the sheets were left untrimmed. It began:

Coach Hiles,

I'm writing you because I can't think of anybody else to tell this to. Like all the other kids on the team what happened to Stacy really bothers me, a lot, even now. There's some things I thought I should tell somebody before I leave here because they might help to find out the truth.

As you probably know, Stacy and I were pretty good friends even though she was a year younger. What I'm trying to say is that before Stacy was kidnapped or whatever she had changed a lot. I don't think anybody else realized just how much she changed and was still changing. It started early last summer.

I never did find out who she was seeing but I got the impression they were older guys and they were getting

---

her to try lots of things, things she was too young to try I'm afraid. I think this because she asked me to lie for her a couple of times (more than a couple) when she wanted to stay out all night with whoever. I can't really say more than that because I don't know the details. She never told me anything specific but I have a feeling that by the fall she had tried pretty much everything. During cross-country we still talked and were sort of friends but not like before (last spring). You remember, I'm sure, how she didn't have that great a season considering what everyone expected from her. Can you guess why? I think I have.

Anyway, near the end of the season she called me late one night and told me she had to see me. This was during the week she was taken. She wanted to meet me right away. I mean that night! So I snuck out and met her and she told me that she was so angry and upset that she just had to talk to a friend. She really didn't say much, but she did mention a journal she had kept all summer and said that if her parents ever found it she'd be in big trouble.

She told me how the book was hidden in the wall of her closet. She said there was a panel down low with screws holding it to the wall. This panel covered up an opening where somebody could get to the bathroom pipes to fix them. The bathroom was next door to her room I guess. The journal is supposed to be on a little ledge above the opening so you have to reach in and up to find it.

You must be wondering why I waited so long to tell anybody about this. The journal I mean. First I was afraid it would be full of bad things, stuff that would hurt her parents. And her reputation. After she disappeared, all the articles in the papers told about how nice and good she was and what a great champion she would have been. I didn't want to hurt anybody. I especially didn't want to hurt such a good friend. So I kept my mouth shut. I guess I always hoped she'd be found and be safe and I thought about how stupid I'd feel if I told anything about the journal and it was bad and it got out and how she would be ruined. Well, it's been a long time now. School for me is just about over.

Coach Hiles, you know I'm not a very strong person. I loved running for your team, and you were nice enough to never say I didn't have what it takes to be very good. I guess I always knew I would never win and be a champion. So this is the best I can do for Stacy. I may be long-gone before you find this, but at least now somebody else knows about the journal, somebody who is strong and will know what to do.

I realize this whole thing was very hard on you too. On you especially. I know you and Stacy were close. She liked and respected you a lot. I just hope I'm not going to cause you too much trouble by telling what I just did. You can do what you think is right. As for me, I'm not going to mention it ever again. Thanks for helping like always.

Lisa Walker

With his heart thudding in slow agonizing beats, his throat tight, his breathing shallow, Marty neatly refolded the letter, slipped it back into its envelope, and slid it underneath the blotter. He switched off the flashlight and sat in the darkness and tried to comprehend what he'd just dis-

---

covered, what he'd just read. Could this be true about the Stacy he'd adored and who adored him? The Stacy he wanted to follow as the Last Goodie? Coach Hiles had said she'd changed, but good god, what had she *done*? After three or four minutes he had relaxed enough to try sneaking back to his room, not sure at all he would sleep well this night either, that he'd ever sleep well again.

Marty pushed the chair away from the desk and stood up. He shuffled cautiously toward the door. He had grabbed the knob and was about to turn it when he saw the thin bar of light along the bottom edge of the door. Oh my god, he thought, afraid he'd inadvertently flicked on a downstairs lamp on his way to the office.

He panicked and yanked the door open but then stepped back so quickly he nearly lost his balance and almost fell. For outside, glowering at him, stood his father.

"Marty, what the hell are you doing?" he asked, not unkindly.

CHAPTER
EIGHT

On Thursday, it took Marty almost three classes to get with it. He'd drifted through math and physics first and second periods and was nearly halfway into third hour before Mr. Warner (English 12) arrested his attention. Marty had been thinking of other things, far more important things than the theme of responsibility in *The Great Gatsby*. He already knew that some people are careless and destructive and that they smash things and then let other people, stronger people, clean up their messes.

So Marty had been only half tuned in to the buzz-buzzing frequency of Mr. Warner's lecture when the narcotic rhythm of the monologue was abruptly shattered. Mr. Warner stopped in the middle of a sentence and stared at the class, scanning the room back and forth, a questioning look changing his features. Finally, when he was sure everyone was paying attention, he asked, "How many of you think this makes any difference, that it means anything?"

"Say what?" someone called from the deep right corner. Laughter rippled across the back of the room.

"This . . . *stuff* we do," continued Warner, "grammar, essays, research, literature. Why should we bother?"

Like most of the other members of the class, Marty had no idea where the discussion would go. This kind of thing had happened once last week and twice the week before, as if, because the school was closing and Mr. Warner's career ending, he felt obliged to consider all the big questions before the tolling of the final bell.

"I don't understand what you want," said Gretchen Thomas, an eager-to-please honor-roll student.

"What I want are honest, thoughtful responses," replied Warner, his dark brown eyes unblinking behind the wire-rimmed glasses, his left hand brushing aside his sandy hair. Marty noticed that, as usual, Warner's tattersall dress shirt was crisp, his burgundy knit tie straight. Even the crease in his poplin slacks was sharp.

"What's the question?" blurted Brian Putman, the no-neck hockey Neanderthal who always, class after class, year after year, wound up sitting behind Marty.

"I asked whether what we do here is important. Does it make any difference?" Warner stepped from behind the lectern and sat on a nearby table, his feet dangling.

"Tell you one thing," began Barry Miller, his normally half-lidded eyes now bright with conviction, "nobody in the real world gives a rip about prepositions and all that. Stuff's got nothin' to do with a job, except maybe gettin' it. And I know what I'm talking about. I been workin' all through high school at lotsa different places."

"Call what you do at Burger Heaven workin'?" teased Putman.

"Oh yeah, Pud-man," answered Miller. "Tell me about it. At least I gotta job. At least I can read a application form. Least I—"

"Wait," interrupted Warner. "Is that it then?" he continued, his voice deep and calm and inviting. "Is that what writing is good for? Getting a job?"

"Isn't it?" someone mumbled.

"What else? Gotta work, right?" said Miller with self-assurance.

"Getting good grades," suggested Gretchen Thomas. "Getting into college."

"'Getting,'" replied Warner thoughtfully. Then he said, "Let me put it this way. Is there anything in writing well . . . *for the writer*? Understand?"

Marty sneaked a look at his classmates. All wore blank expressions, most staring at their desk tops.

"What I mean is . . . is writing something you only do for somebody else? To get something? Or can there be something in it for you, the writer?"

"It helps you think better," said Princeton-bound Eddie Binelli, easily the most talented writer in the group. "You're sort of forced to make connections and see things as they are, if you're honest."

"Are writing and grammar one and the same?" Warner asked Binelli.

"No," Eddie said conclusively.

"No," confirmed Warner. "Can you elaborate, Eddie?"

"No," he said simply.

Warner and Marty laughed. "May I elaborate?" Warner asked the class.

"Be my guest," said Binelli.

"Listen please. This is something you should remem-

---

ber." He paused for effect, then began. "Writing can be a way of learning, of coming to know. It's doing something to the world around you. Ordering it. Getting control of it. In fact, the way you see things, how you arrange them—that's who you are, that's your perspective. So writing can be a way of putting yourself together. A self-creating process."

Warner stopped. He was staring at the floor now, lost in thought. He quickly looked up, made eye contact with Marty, then shifted his gaze to someone else. "Does anybody know what the hell I'm talking about?" he asked.

"Does anybody care?" mumbled Putman.

Marty tensed. He respected Warner and had no time for Putman. He was feeling suddenly rankled, taut, even violent, atypical impulses at 10:25 in the morning.

"Let me try once more," said Warner, apparently not hearing Putman's aside. He took a deep breath, pursed his lips. "Learning spelling, punctuation, grammar, and sentence styling," he said, "is like learning drilling, sawing, sanding, and finishing in shop class. You can practice those skills forever if you want to, but sooner or later it comes time to make something, something good enough to take home.

"Writing is like that. It's a way for you to make something worth keeping. And that something . . . is yourself. So it's a way of saving yourself, winning yourself back from whatever threatens to enslave you or even destroy you. It comes down to this: life can happen to you, or you can happen to life."

"Heyyyyyy, now that's heavy," Putman muttered sarcastically. "Real pro-found."

At that point Marty had had enough. He turned around, scowled at Putman, who slouched arrogantly. Marty said

---

quietly, evenly, "If you shut up, I *won't* shove a puck through your nose."

They locked stares.

"Sure thing, Martina. You're just the guy to do it." Putman started to sit up and reach for Marty when Marty slipped his fists under the front edge of Putman's desk and jerked it up. The desk lifted, throwing Putman off-balance, tossing him into the chair back, his arms flailing comically. Marty held the desk off the floor, his biceps popping with hatred.

"Marty?" called Warner.

"I wanna do it, Putman," Marty said, meaning tip the desk all the way back, dump Putman on his can, maybe break his neck.

"Mr. Oliver!" said Warner, louder this time.

"Why? Because your little buddy Harper beat you out?" said Putman, still awkwardly at bay. That got Marty's attention and Putman knew it. "No star no more, huh?" Putman added, sneering.

Marty felt the blood rush up his neck and explode in his face. He let the desk go and turned around. He didn't see Putman pitch forward and smash his left foot beneath a dropping desk leg.

"Stop it!" hollered Warner, who seldom raised his voice. "What's happening to you people? Marty?"

Marty shrugged, shook his head once.

"Go on, star. Tell 'em," said Putman in a gritty whisper, leaning into the aisle, rubbing his injured foot. "You're a has-been."

Before Marty could reply, Warner ordered the class to be silent and take out their novels and study guides. "Finish another chapter's worth of questions," he said. "I think

---

it would do us all some good to meditate quietly for the rest of the hour. And work."

When the class had settled into the routine of filling out worksheets, Marty tried to focus his mind on something besides the rage he felt. He wanted to ignore Putman, forget him, so he re-created the conversation he'd had last night with his father. They'd talked about some writing that had made a difference, only this writing unsettled everyone, brought chaos to order.

"I knew sooner or later you would read it," his father had said after catching Marty red-handed and red-faced in the office. "I just wish you'd let me share things with you instead of . . . stealing them."

Marty had nodded, agreeing, then hung his head. He'd asked, "What does it all mean?"

"It means I've already called Eldon Taggert."

"The detective from before?"

"And there when I need him, too."

"He knows about Stacy?"

"All about her. And if he's still good, he's already got the paperwork done that'll get him, us, into Stacy's old house to look for the journal."

"You think it's still there?"

"We'll find out tomorrow. And I'll even share that with you. Despite this poor showing."

Marty had looked up, smiled. "Yeah?"

"Trust me, okay?" They'd exchanged looks. Then Marty's father had continued, "I guess I shouldn't complain about your resourcefulness and powers of observation. It's kind of fun to see you scratch up evidence. And it's easier to let you do that with Mom gone, if you know what I mean. Maybe, finally, we can get this thing resolved without having her get upset. It's hardly consoling, but it is a small benefit from her being away."

"I know."

"As for now, get it to bed, or you won't even be able to handle a light workout. I just hope all these coincidences and revelations won't ruin your concentration over the long run."

The bell ending English brought Marty back from his reverie. He shuffled out of the room with his semicomatose classmates, feeling only mildly concerned about the "bottom line" of Mr. Warner's philosophical excursion, feeling even less concerned about Brian Putman. Still, Marty decided to wait just outside the door in case Putman wanted to push things. You don't run from guys like that, Marty realized. It would be worse then. But when Putman emerged, he shot past Marty and shouldered his way into the hall traffic. Marty watched him go before taking off in the opposite direction. He hoped that was the end of it.

The rest of the day passed quickly and uneventfully, and soon Marty was dressing for his last practice before regions on Saturday. Friday workouts before big meets were so light they hardly qualified as practice sessions. And Coach Hiles had cut back on his scheduled training so much that today's practice for Marty would be much like Friday's.

About halfway through the practice, Harper approached Marty. Ted hadn't spoken to him since the accident, and his lack of concern confused Marty. But Ted was Ted. Unpredictable.

Harper quietly asked, "You really okay?"

"Guess so," Marty replied.

"I didn't trip you, did I? I'm sure I didn't bump you at all. I was a full stride behind you."

"You didn't. I stepped on the curb."

Ted stared silently at him.

"Anyway," Marty continued, ending the embarrassing silence, "I was dying. Big Bear was on my back. Falling might have been fated."

"Yeah," said Harper, nodding sagely. "Maybe that's it."

Marty looked away.

"You're not going to challenge, huh? Coach just told me."

Marty shook his head.

"You're really going to settle for the second spot."

"Uh-huh."

"I don't believe it."

"Believe it."

"Your idea?"

Marty nodded. "Mostly," he said, smiling. He was sure Harper wasn't trying to psych him out or humiliate him or bait him. He assumed Harper simply wanted him to confirm the startling fact that for the first time in his high school career Ted was running as Southwestern's number-one miler.

"Listen," continued Harper, "I hope you realize this isn't personal, okay?"

"Hey, it's no big—"

"It's just that I'm sick of it," interrupted Harper. "Understand? Remember that, okay?"

Before Marty could reply, Harper turned and ran off. They didn't talk again for the rest of practice. By the time Marty completed his light workout, he was more than anxious to get home and find out what his father had accomplished.

At home that afternoon, Marty found no one to answer his questions. His father had gone off without leaving him a note—a rare omission. When Marty checked his dad's office, he was surprised to see the usually chaotic desk top had been cleaned, the carelessly tossed papers neatly arranged in little piles, a sizable work area cleared of debris. Such conscientious maintenance usually meant one thing: Ken Oliver was about to start writing a longer, more important piece, a major article or book outline.

Marty left the office, climbed the stairs, and entered his room. He would rest and wait it out. His father always came back, always kept him informed, always was there. His mother, on the other hand . . . was away. Two steps into his room were all Marty needed to find proof of his dad's reliability. The inevitable note was on Marty's desk, covering a stack of photocopied sheets. Marty picked up the letter and read:

Marty,

We got the journal! It was relatively easy because the house was empty, up for sale again. The journal was damp and dirty but readable, still hidden in the wall. We scanned it and found out some things we wanted to know. Found more than we wanted, actually. I've made copies of the most telling pages. I'm sorry, but after reading them you'll see Stacy differently. She was a different girl from what we all knew. She'd hit bottom. These entries explain her behavior near the end. They'll upset you. She chose to throw away everything, but what's really maddening is how this O. C. (whoever he is) helped her do it. I'll be home by 9:30 tonight.

Love, Dad

P.S. Obviously, you're not to show these papers to anyone.

Marty threw his books on the bed, pulled out the desk chair, and sat down. With trembling hands, he picked up the excerpts.

CHAPTER
NINE

He looked over the first of the sheets and noticed the handwriting was careful, uniform, and obviously feminine. The journal entry before him was dated June 9, the beginning of the summer following Stacy's sophomore year, a summer nearly twelve years gone. Marty picked up the pages and began reading:

Just like always, I got into an argument with Mike that pretty much ruined the evening. He's cute and fun but for a senior he's such a baby sometimes. And so possessive. I suppose you could say we're going together since neither of us have gone out with anybody else for the last month, but I guess I don't really like him as much as he likes me. That's the trouble. Isn't it always? If you show any interest at all in a guy he either runs away to mommy, scared out of his mind, or he thinks you're ready to do anything he asks. Like this evening. Everything was going okay. The show was fun. Afterwards, just before sundown, we went to the lake (Harriet) for a walk. We had just started down the path when O. C. came jogging by. I don't think Mike knows him, but O. C. stopped anyway and talked to us awhile. As soon as he took off again, Mike asked me if I liked him or something. I said, Are you kidding? But he kept right at it. He said he could tell O. C. would like to take me out and then he asked me if I'd go. At that point I'd had it. So I decided to tease Mike a little. Gee, I don't know, I said. O. C. is awfully cute and I like the way he runs, I said. Of course stupid Mike doesn't realize I'm joking. He said (trying to be so cool) Look, if you can't be loyal at all, if I can't trust you, I'm going to . . . You're going to what, I asked. You're MINE! he yelled then so loud that some older people walking ahead of us stopped and turned around. I just looked at Mike and shook my head and laughed. Needless to say, that did it. About two weeks ago the same kind of thing happened and he grabbed my arm and told me never never to laugh at him, ever. He takes himself so damn seriously I guess. When he started to grab my arm again (like before) I pulled it away and told him not to touch me like that or I'd scream. Well, screw you, you little uppity bitch! he said. (And I'm afraid that's about as clever with words as any guy at Southwestern can get.) So then he started walking away. I suppose he expected me to run after him and beg him to touch me all over and to please please forgive me for everything! But I didn't move. At all. He stopped a couple of times on the way back up to his car like he was giving me another chance to think about what a great guy I was losing. I just let him go. Finally, he gets in his car and squeals away up the hill as if that proves something. I kept standing there thinking how stupid the whole scene was and pretty soon I started giggling. Laughing ac-

tually, out loud. I didn't feel bad about being left at Lake Harriet because even though it's supposed to be dangerous after the sun goes down I had jogged there from my house lots of times and knew I could be home in twenty minutes if I ran. The trouble was I had on nice slacks and clogs. No jogging tonight, I concluded. I was just about to start walking it home when who should show up behind me but O. C. Is anything wrong, he asked. Not anymore, I answered. O. C. laughed and asked what had happened to Mike. When I told him he laughed again and offered me a ride home. A block before we got there he pulled over to the curb and said, Well, what about it? What about what, I said. If I asked you out would you go with me? We could play racquets at the club, he said. I thought about it for maybe two seconds and said sure. You know I like older guys, I said. He laughed again and touched my arm. How much older, he asked. His green eyes were glittering, I think.

Marty wasted no time moving to the next excerpt. This one was dated June 28, almost three weeks later. It began:

Tonight O. C. said he's never met anyone like me. He says I'm different and special and pretty and a million other things I suppose I shouldn't believe. Like always, I had to lie to M & D and tell them I was staying out late with Lori and Lisa and going to some all-girl party that didn't exist. I can't even remember now exactly what I said. I just hope they (Lori and Lisa) are both out of town like they said they'd be. In fact, I had to tell M & D I was staying real late because O. C. said that after racquets (he always calls the game "racquets" because he says it's such a "beau-

---

tiful front for so many enterprises and special friend-
ships"), anyway, he said that after we played he wanted to
do something special to celebrate our three-week anniver-
sary. What he wanted to do was go out to Lake Minnetonka
and park and talk. We raced out there afterwards and it
was already very dark. He can drive like a race car driver
so we made it in record time I'm sure. He knew right where
we could go to be alone and look at the lake and watch the
rich people having parties on their sailboats and motor
yachts that were all lighted up. We drove down a gravel
road between two great big mansions. More like estates,
really. Once we were parked he told me that ever since the
day he showed up to help out with the guys team and saw
me running he'd wanted to meet me. But he couldn't do
anything right there at school. He said he knew all about
me from the articles in the paper. I guess I just sort of
smiled and took it all in. He told me he knew my phone
number and where I lived and how much he had wanted to
call but was always afraid to because he felt funny, being so
much older than me. Anyway, he was full of compliments
and the night was beautiful and when he kissed me I felt all
tingly. I thought something was about to explode inside.
He was sooooo different from Mike that I can't even begin
to describe how much. I let him touch me but it didn't
seem bad or wrong. He was very careful and sensitive so it
felt good. We planned to meet again for racquets the day
after tomorrow. I guess I'm going to be a prisoner of desire
or something. I hope so. It's late now and I'm tired but I
think if I keep writing I'll be able to work my way right
through tomorrow and get back to basics with O. C. (Oh
shameless me!)

P.S. Mom left me a note saying that Mike called.
UGH!! What a little immature baby.

The next sheet was dated July 11. Marty read:

Well, I guess I'm in over my head now. It finally happened. I suppose I knew it would considering the way things have been going for the last month. Our racquet games were getting shorter and shorter and our make-out trips longer and longer. Anyway, last night O. C. had me set it up so I could be out all night. I told M & D I was sleeping at Lisa's. I'm amazed they haven't caught me lying yet. One phone call would do it. I really should tell Lisa what's going on since she's my best friend right now. She must know I'll tell her everything someday. I'm sure she thinks something very unusual is happening to me but she doesn't know what. For me it's frightening to be so trusted, I guess, by your parents, and friends. I thought once I should come clean and tell them EVERYTHING! But now I can see what a dumb move that would have been. So there we were out at Minnetonka as usual and O. C. was all over me and as usual I was liking it because we were both high. With O. C. I've gotten into drinking wine and doing some other things that aren't half as bad as I was told they were. He says a little recreational use like this hasn't hurt his game. He still plays well enough to keep his job, he said. Finally, after we both were so turned on we couldn't stand it anymore he said, Why don't you come over to my place for the night. It's not too far from here. Where is it, I asked. Not far at all, he said and he started backing up the car. I fixed myself up and smiled at him and he drove us to the highway. We passed some restaurants and condominiums and apartments all built along the shoreline and pretty soon we came to a little bitty cottage set way back off the road in the trees. It was somebody's summer place years and years ago but now to get to the lake from it you

---

have to cross the highway and three parking lots and then ask permission from the owners of all those places to put your feet on their precious beach.

We parked behind the cottage and went in. It smelled musty and dirty but it was kind of cute too. We smoked another joint and drank some more wine and then he showed me his room. I laughed and pretty soon he laughed because it looked like a little kid's bedroom. He said it was decorated that way when he moved in a few months ago. The wallpaper was the best. It made you feel like you were in a zoo because all the way around the room from the floor to the ceiling there were long black stripes like bars and behind them were big colorful pictures of bears and elephants and giraffes and lions and tigers. After a while it seemed like the animals were outside the bars and I was on the inside. Like an optical illusion. Welcome to the lion's den, he said as he pulled me over for a kiss. I laughed again. I couldn't believe I was doing what I was doing. I was being very bad and knew I was going to be worse. But I was feeling so good I couldn't help myself. I wish I could say I fainted or something and don't remember what happened. But I do remember. And I wanted it to happen. And he knew I wanted it to, and like always he was very careful and gentle. As I think about it tonight (the day after) I realize how much I just wanted to experience it. I wanted to know what it felt like, that's all. I just wanted to KNOW. When it was over, I was all warm and soft and relaxed and he couldn't believe it was my first time. We slept and I didn't feel guilty or ashamed at all. What's the matter with me? Anyway, I'm sure it won't be my last time. I'm so weak and he's so strong. Later, I woke up and it was still night and O. C. was sitting up next to me smoking. I got up and we shared the joint and pretty soon we both started

---

feeling silly so we decided to have a caption contest. For the rest of the night we went running around his little bedroom with Magic Markers drawing big circles near the animals' heads and connecting the animal and his thought with strings of smaller circles. In the big circles we wrote what we imagined the animals were thinking while they watched us. "Ooo-la-la!" O. C. wrote in the circle next to a winking hippo.

Before we split up I asked O. C. if he didn't ever want to do things with other people, maybe his friends. He said, Baby, what we got going is serious business—legally, you know? It seemed silly when he said it—that just because I'm a minor and he's older we shouldn't be together. But I guess for now maybe he's right. My parents would scream if they knew I was going out with O. C. And if any of my friends knew, M & D would find out eventually for sure.

The following installment was written almost six weeks after the previous excerpt.

How could I be so stupid? Why didn't I see that Mike wasn't an exception at all. His immaturity and selfishness is just typical of guys, I'm afraid. At least that's what this girl has learned. I discovered it today when I told O. C. about my (our) problem. He told me he couldn't believe I wasn't taking anything. He said he thought I was a little more responsible than that, and mature enough to take care of such things. He said it was all my fault for not telling him. When I tried to say the same things back to him he started yelling and he hit me. I mean he slapped me so hard I lost my balance. I fell down and started crying. He kept right on yelling. He said things like, I don't care

---

how old you are, you're old enough to know you can't be doing what we've been doing all summer without protection. I thought about screaming back, Well what about you!?! But I knew if I said that he'd probably hit me again. Big man. All I wanted was to get away from there fast. He sat down in a chair and sulked. I mean he pouted like a five-year-old. What are we going to do about it, I asked. What do you mean WE, he said. Then he said, You got yourself in trouble by being stupid. You can't expect me to think for you ALL the time. I'm not cleaning up YOUR messes. Then we were quiet for a minute and I spent the time thinking how I wasn't ready at all to be a mother or to be married to anybody, especially an irresponsible baby like O. C. I just wasn't old enough for all that. Get an abortion, he said finally. Where, I asked. There's all kinds of clinics, he said. Just tell them you're on welfare or a runaway or something. I said, They won't believe that. Will you pay for it then? That's when O. C. told me I was crazy and I should get out of his place. When I told him I couldn't walk home, he got up and grabbed me by the arm and pulled me out of the cottage. I don't know what time it was but it must have been very late because nobody was out. Without saying anything, he pushed me into his car and then went around and got in himself. He was spinning his tires all the way up to the highway. He raced back to the city and took me to the end of my block and after he pulled over to the curb he reached across me and pushed open my door. He never said a word. He just sat there looking straight ahead. Just before I got out I started crying. I couldn't help it. I never felt so alone. I looked at him once more and he was scowling, trying to look tough I guess. Finally, he just shoved me out of the car and yanked the door shut and roared away. I hated him then like I never hated anyone.

84

Marty hurriedly moved on to a short entry dated August 28. It read:

Next week school starts. I was supposed to be practicing with the cross-country team for over two weeks now but I told Coach Hiles I wasn't feeling well. He told me to come out when I felt better. He didn't even ask when that might be, or what was wrong but just to do some light exercise to keep in shape. I guess he trusts me too. The trouble is, I don't know if I'll ever feel better. Two days ago I went to the People's Clinic downtown. I went there all by myself even though at the last minute I called Lisa and tried to make myself ask her to go with me. She knew something was really terribly wrong but I just couldn't bring myself to tell her everything. The less people who know about this the better, I figure. After I hung up I felt happy to know Lisa was there if I needed her. I can't say the same for O. C. At the clinic they asked me for "a name." Not my name really. It seemed pretty clear they wanted nothing but a phony name for the record. Besides, I bet fake names must cut down quite a bit on phone calls from angry parents. Whatever. After the doctor was through I felt completely depressed and deserted like there was absolutely nobody who could talk to me and say anything worth hearing. I tried not to think about what I'd done. I cried. The nurses were smart enough not to say too much to me and the doctor only said to relax and wait for the pain to pass. While I was in the recovery room I felt so ashamed and abandoned that for a while I hated myself almost more than I hated O. C.

Then, on September 17, Stacy wrote:

I think I got him good, maybe. I think he'll squirm and after a while I can be even with him. I decided it would only be right for him to feel as bad as I've felt for the past few weeks. For starters I sent him a little note. In it I said I was ready to tell my dad about what happened last summer. I told O. C. my dad would make a lot of trouble for him if he didn't own up and help me right now. I never said anything about my visit to the clinic so I was hoping I could really scare him. But I sent the letter almost two weeks ago and he hasn't said anything yet. I guess I'll have to think of something even better. By the way, cross-country is going okay now. Coach Hiles still hasn't said anything about my "slow start" this fall. I just hope to god he never finds out about all this mess I've made for myself.

Finally, Marty came to the last page his father had deemed worth reading. The date at the top was only two days before Stacy's kidnapping. His father had written in the upper left-hand corner, "This is the final installment." Marty picked it up and read:

Today I outdid myself. I think I'll really get even with this brilliant move. I sent him another note and told him I'd written a long summary of everything he'd done to me and everything I knew about him, how he was cheating the club. I said the report was ready to go in the mail. I told him copies would go to the club, the police, his new girlfriend, my father, anybody that could reveal what he was. I even claimed I found some witnesses that would say they saw him pushing me around and hurting me. Of course, this was all BS but it sure sounded scary. I scared myself writing it. At the end I said I would throw away all that stuff if he would pay me $3,000. I knew the one threat that would get him was sending my "report" to the club because that was where he usually picked up his girlfriends (the

---

stupid idiots). And the police, he was always scared of the police. I'm pretty sure he was dealing as well as using but I can't say for certain because I never actually saw him do it. Maybe that's why he hung around the school and practices so much even when his workouts were done. Anyway, I've decided if he does send the money I'm either going to burn it or cut it into little pieces and send it back to him. But then again, I don't know. Maybe I'll see just how much I can get out of him. That would be fun. I sent the letter before noon so he should get it in a day or two if the creep is even still in town.

(An hour later) I can't help thinking about a talk I had with Lisa almost a month ago (when everything with O. C. was going bad). It didn't seem that important or insightful then but now I find myself hearing parts of the conversation over and over. I said to Lisa that I always thought there were rules, absolute rules. Rules nobody could break because there are some things you just couldn't do, shouldn't ever do. Lisa agreed with me. She agreed there are rules like that. Then I said, NO. Unh-uh. There aren't! I found that out this summer. I know now you can do any damn thing you want. The people who keep talking about rules are people who want to shut you up and control you and dominate you. Lisa said, You mean parents? I said, Parents, teachers, preachers, coaches, the whole crowd. Then Lisa said, But Stacy you have to have rules. They help you to control yourself so you don't hurt anybody else. So you won't hurt yourself. I didn't talk for a few seconds and then I said, Yeah, Lisa, I like that. That's good. But know what? I'm the one who's going to make the rules for me. I'm not going to take them secondhand from some grown-up. I'm going to test them, try out the rules personally before I accept any of them.—Now as I think about

---

*it I don't know if that was the smartest thing I ever said . . .
or the dumbest.*

*I just thought of something else. I bet I told O. C. about
this journal, how I keep it in the garage. I'm sure I did. I
should probably move it. You know, I just wish I could talk
to someone right now. I really haven't talked with Lisa
since that time a month ago. There's so much inside me,
but I don't know how much I could ever tell. I only know I
could use a friend right now.*

After he'd finished reading, Marty sat for a long time staring at the crisp photocopies. He was numb and silent and
disoriented. This wasn't his Stacy, no way, no how.

Eventually, he glanced at his watch, noted the time, and
decided to distract himself with homework until his father
returned. Hopefully his dad would have some answers,
some explanation of why all this had to happen to Stacy. As
Marty opened his math book, he realized that waiting is the
hardest thing you ever have to do.

CHAPTER
TEN

On Friday, as Marty marched mechanically through another all-too-typical week-ending battery of tests and quizzes, he began hearing rumors of war—what the members of the senior class planned to do to sabotage the last week of Southwestern's educational life. As much as Marty wanted to join in those illicit discussions and offer a few cute stratagems of his own, he was obsessed to the point of distraction by what his father had told him last night. He was so bewildered that he uncharacteristically failed his first two quizzes.

Ken Oliver hadn't come home until nearly eleven o'clock that night. But when he did arrive he was so full of news it took an hour-long rapid-fire monologue to summarize the rest of Stacy's journal. Marty could hardly believe the explicit, gut-wrenching narratives were written by, let alone directly experienced by, the same innocent and energetic girl who once challenged him to foot races across the front lawn and around his backyard.

Even though Marty's father had spent most of the evening with Detective Eldon Taggert, there was no word yet on a positive identification for O. C. If they ever discovered who O. C. was and where he was and what he was, Marty vowed he would personally kick hell out of him, kick him into hell, if the guy wasn't there already. Even if O. C. wasn't the one who'd taken Stacy, Marty wanted to kick him anyway for what he did to her before she disappeared.

For his last practice before regions (the local meets from which state-meet finalists emerge), Marty was given an extremely light workout. Throughout the short session, Ted Harper went out of his way to encourage Marty. Without thinking, with no hesitation, Marty reciprocated. They finished practice typically, talking and joking.

Still, something had changed, something far more subtle than their rankings. And they both realized it. Marty saw it in Harper's eyes, and knew that tomorrow they would give each other a race unlike any they'd ever run.

When Marty got home he was greeted by another note from his father. It began:

Marty,

Make yourself supper. There's some fresh thin-sliced roast beef in the refrigerator. I'll be back much earlier than last night—Promise! But I'll probably be bringing some familiar faces with me. Without a doubt you'll be asked to join us, so stay dressed and looking presentable.

See ya, Dad

At 8:10 P.M. Ken Oliver hurried into the house, concentrating on the little notebook he held open in his right hand. Marty had bounded down the stairs two at a time and barely asked, "What's up?" when his father waved him off and muttered, as he headed for his office, "Let me organize my notes for a few minutes. When everybody's here I'll go through it. Sorry, no preview."

Marty watched his father disappear into his office and pull the door closed behind him. By now Marty had come to recognize phrases like "I'm organizing my notes" or "I'm trying to straighten out some ideas" or "I've got to get this down while it's fresh" as pleas—demands—for complete silence and consideration. Marty no longer felt neglected or belittled by these requests. They were simply a part of life when your dad was a writer who did lots of his work at home. Marty wandered into the family room, grabbed a magazine, sat down and began reading.

About twenty minutes after Ken Oliver had sequestered himself, the doorbell rang. Marty answered it and was startled to find his coach on the front steps.

"Surprised?" Hiles asked. "Don't think I'm spying, okay? Your dad tell you to expect me?"

Marty shook his head. Hiles laughed as he came in. Marty glanced at the office door. It remained shut, so entertaining Coach Hiles would be Marty's responsibility for at least a few minutes. However, before Marty led his coach into the living room, the doorbell sounded again. This time Marty was more than surprised. He was awed. Detective Eldon Taggert had arrived.

Taggert seemed intimidating to Marty because he looked so much like a brutal TV cop. He had chillingly cold, unblinking pale blue eyes, a thin mouth, beefy shoulders, hairy hands, and a rumpled sport coat.

"Hi, kid," Taggert said. "You know how tired I am of

getting this message?" He handed a note to Marty who read the OFFICIAL DEPARTMENT MEMO. On it was written, "E.T. phone home." Marty laughed, and the intimidation diminished as Taggert stepped inside. Marty was about to introduce Taggert and Coach Hiles when Ken Oliver emerged from his office.

Ignoring everyone but Eldon Taggert, Marty's dad asked, "You get anything?"

"Enough," Taggert replied, a little smile tightening the muscles around his mouth.

Ken looked questioningly at Taggert, but the detective said no more. Marty's father shrugged, realized that for now Taggert wasn't talking. He decided to organize the meeting. The four of them walked to the family room, Taggert and Ken carrying notebooks and pens.

When they were comfortably seated, Marty's dad began. "To give ourselves a sense of direction, Eldon and I thought we should talk to everyone close to the case as soon as possible. We spent the day calling around and getting statements. As for the journal, we're still the only ones who know it exists and what's in it. And that's how it's got to stay.

"Here's what we have so far. We figure O. C. was some kind of part-time coach at Southwestern or one of the schools Southwestern regularly played against. He was probably a tennis coach. Stacy's many references to 'racquets' make that the obvious choice. Were you able to get anything from Bruce Skuppers, Eldon?"

Instead of answering, Taggert looked at Hiles and said, "Has that jackass Skuppers really been a principal for twenty years?"

Hiles grinned and nodded.

"What do you think of him?" asked Taggert. "That a fair question?"

"What's to think?" said Hiles. "He's typical."

"Oh, he's more than that. Don't sell him short. He could be the most incoherent and paranoid mealy-mouth I've ever questioned."

Marty struggled to suppress a laugh. Skuppers's fear of controversy, his fear of students, his nearly incapacitating fear of parents, were all common knowledge at Southwestern.

Ken Oliver said, "He wasn't much help?"

"Help!? The first thing he says after I identify myself and tell him I want information on an assistant coach of his was . . . wait a sec, it's here in my notes. Yeah, got it. He said, 'Let me say that first of all every one of our coaches are properly certified and operating within the clearly defined contractual parameters of supervisory responsibility vis-à-vis any potential liability claims with regard to athletic safety concerns.'" Taggert looked up, pulled at his ear, and scanned his audience for clarification, a translation.

"What did you say to that?" Hiles asked.

"I asked him what the hell he was talking about. I told him I wasn't a recruiter for the Defense Department but just trying for a lead on an assistant tennis coach who might've worked for him eleven, twelve years ago. Told him to speak English."

"And?"

"When I mentioned the initials *O. C.* nothing registered. And I mean nothing. He just referred me to the athletic director, who, of course, was gone for the day."

"What about you, John?" asked Ken. "Any ideas?"

Hiles cleared his throat. "I sort of remember a guy who came in maybe one or two days a week to work with both the girls' and boys' tennis teams."

"What'd he look like?" Taggert asked, notebook up, pen ready.

"That's what's vague. I think he was a handsome guy, tall with long black hair, maybe a moustache. But when I went through all the old team pictures and yearbooks today, I couldn't find him anyplace."

"Glasses? Scars? Two left feet?" asked Taggert.

"Don't know. Sorry."

"Who was the head coach then? He still around?"

"No. He moved to Texas about five years ago. Got out of the business. Guy named Jerry Ebert."

"John," said Marty's dad, "while I think of it, I have to ask you this. Don't be offended, okay?"

"Must be bad. Shoot."

"How is it possible that an intelligent and sensitive coach like you could've had no idea what Stacy was doing?"

Hiles waited for a few moments before answering. "I knew something wasn't right," he began. "I knew she'd changed, but I never imagined she'd covered so much ground in such a hurry. Now, of course, I can't see how I missed it. That was the way she did things. Lots of ground in a big damn hurry. It should've been obvious, right? She pushed herself past the limit as fast as she could. You can see why she didn't pick a partner her own age."

"Why?" Marty asked.

"She didn't want a relationship. She wanted experience. Like she said, she just 'wanted to know.' Too bad she forgot that adult games can have adult consequences."

"Um," said Taggert.

"But I didn't suspect anything like what we found in the journal, if it's true."

"Why wouldn't it be?" asked Ken.

"Kids, you know, like to dramatize themselves. It could be exaggeration, imagination."

"Eldon?"

"I think it's probably true," Taggert said. "I had a nice talk about it with Lisa Walker, now Mrs. Lisa Holland, a legal secretary in Clearwater, Florida. Went there right after high school when her dad was transferred." Taggert was reading from his notes. "Anyway," he continued, "she was absolutely stunned when I called. She figured John had found her letter years ago and decided to ignore it. Thought maybe he'd looked for the journal and missed it, or if he got it, decided it was useless. Whatever had happened, she thought she'd done her duty, all she could."

"Had she ever read it?"

"No. In the letter she'd said she never actually saw it and she confirmed that. But she remembered the call Stacy writes about making just before she visited the clinic. And she remembers meeting her that October night just before Stacy was taken."

"Did you tell her we have the journal?"

"Uh-huh. And I told her not to discuss it with anyone but me."

"She agree?" Ken asked.

"Yes."

"Good."

"I also said I'd keep her name out of things altogether, and she was happy for that. She's still trying to forget."

"Did she know anything about O. C.?" Hiles asked.

"Nothing. She said during that summer she saw very

little of Stacy although they talked a lot on the phone. Stacy was 'always busy.' Lisa remembered a few times when Stacy asked her to cover for her, but she couldn't remember specific dates."

"Great," muttered Hiles.

The four of them sat glumly. "O. C." was still just a sound, not a name, a specific person.

Taggert asked, "What about the Davises, Ken?"

Marty looked quickly at his dad.

"It wasn't easy to find them. There are about fifty Jim Davises or J. Davises in the Minneapolis book alone. I tried calling the company he repped for when he lived in the neighborhood, but they're out of business. So I went down the list of fifty and got nowhere. Then I realized Jim and Kathy's number might still be unlisted. Like us, they just about went crazy with crank calls. Guys asking for ransom, drunks telling stories about seeing Stacy in New York, Times Square—stuff like that. All pretty sick.

"Next I tried local companies that made the kinds of electrical components Jim had sold. Fifteen or twenty calls later, bingo! I got a Jim Davis in the right age category with vaguely the right looks and an unlisted number in Deep Haven, which I sweet-talked out of the secretary.

"When I called, Kathy answered. She almost hung up on me. Thought I was another wise guy. After I calmed her down, she agreed to call Jim and we set up a meeting for this afternoon."

"When you mentioned the journal . . ." Taggert said, prompting Ken.

"I know what you're thinking."

"Yeah? What?"

"They might want to suppress it."

"Exactly. Where'd you go with that?"

"I said it would be a crucial piece of evidence if we hoped to find, arrest, and prosecute O. C."

"They want to see it?"

"I stalled them there."

"How?"

"I told them you had it, the police."

"And they'll sit still?"

"All they asked was to be given the journal if O. C. can't be found."

"What'd you say?"

"I agreed, Eldon. What else could I do?"

"Nothing, I suppose. You told them not to say anything about it?"

"I didn't have to. Jim was way ahead of me. He promised to keep everything confidential."

"I don't imagine they got us any closer to O. C.," said Hiles.

"No."

Taggert sighed loudly.

Ken Oliver continued, "They'd been suspicious about Stacy's activities that summer but decided her aimlessness was just another phase."

"How are they doing?" Hiles thought to ask.

"Three years ago they nearly divorced. I guess they got some good counseling just in time. It'll never be over for them no matter what we do."

"Did they give you *anything* that relates to O. C.?" Taggert asked, his voice finally betraying a glimmer of impatience.

"One big thing."

"Which was?"

"I asked Kathy if Stacy had shown an interest in tennis that summer, and she remembered one time when Stacy left the house at night she had a borrowed racquet. Kathy asked her about it, and Stacy said she couldn't possibly play at such a classy place as the Metro without prestige equipment."

"The Metro? What—tennis club?" replied Taggert as he flipped through his notes. "Never heard of that one. And I've called 'em all, everything in the seven-county area." He looked up from his notebook. "The Metro," he repeated, and then wrote it down.

"What have we got? Anything?" asked Marty's father.

"Not much," said Taggert, "until we find a black-haired part-time coach who once worked at or worked-out at the Metro."

"Wait a minute," said Hiles. "What about this Mike, the boyfriend Stacy mentions in the journal?"

Again Taggert flipped through his notes. "Already called him," replied Taggert. "Here it is. Mike Brenner. Said he doesn't remember the Lake Harriet scene very well, and swears he never knew anybody called O. C."

"Did you remind him? Press him?"

"Sure."

"And?"

"He said he was going to break up with her that night anyway. O. C. showing up just made it easier, gave him a handy excuse."

"Nice guy."

"I think he's being straight with us though. He didn't follow tennis at school, he never saw O. C. before, and was never introduced."

"Marty," said Ken Oliver, "anything you want to add?"

Marty cleared his throat. "Well, I've been listening to the tapes we made and I found something I wanted to ask you about."

"What?"

"On an early one, when you asked me what I heard, you know, what Stacy screamed, I said it sounded like 'No—gee—skurd.' But when I wrote that essay last year, without looking back or even thinking much about it, I said it sounded like 'No—tsee—hurt.'"

"No-gee . . . no-gee . . . no-tsee . . . O. C.?" suggested Taggert. "You buy it?" he asked, squinting at Ken Oliver.

"That's using your imagination," answered Marty's dad. Then turning to his son he commented, "You always said, even at the start, you felt she was screaming to you, trying to tell you something."

"Hurt. Skurd. What the hell do we do with that, even if she was saying O. C.?" asked Taggert. "Suggestions?"

"My god," mumbled Hiles, sitting up quickly. "I just thought of something."

Everyone turned toward him.

"The boys' tennis coach this year at Westview Junior High, one of our feeder schools, was a classmate of Stacy's. I remember because he came out for track during the indoor season, but then quit to play tennis once the weather improved. That was his best sport."

"Call him," ordered Taggert.

"Now?"

"Why not?"

Hiles got up. "Phone book?" he asked.

Ken directed him to the one in his office, and the three of them—Ken, Marty, and Taggert—waited silently as Hiles placed the call. Hiles came back a few minutes later and said the ex-Southwestern player, Tom Dvorak, recalled a part-time coach named Curt something. A real jerk, too. Dvorak didn't think he ever knew the guy's last name. But he remembered that he always showed up wearing expensive monogrammed tennis whites with green letters on the sleeves—"

"The letters?" interrupted Taggert.

"MTRC."

"What'd they stand for?"

"Metro Tennis and Racquet Club. I asked Tom if he knew anything about the place. He said he played there a couple of times before it burned down. It used to be on South France Avenue."

"Great!" whispered Taggert, writing frantically in his notebook. "What'd you say the kid's name was?"

"The guy I just talked to?"

"Him and the yo-yo we're trying to peg as O. C."

"I called Tom Dvorak, and O. C. is Curt somebody."

"Curt . . . hurt . . . skurd," mumbled Taggert over and over.

After everyone had gone, Marty lay awake in bed thinking about Stacy. He let his mind drift, tried to recreate other moments from other times with her. Like a ritual chant he began slowly repeating the letters O-C, O-C, O-C. . . .

Eventually, when he was halfway between sleep and waking, it came to him, her voice, a scene, more than a dream. He was small. They were watching *The Wizard* . . . the yellow brick road that leads to . . . to . . . Oz.

She said, "Oz . . . Would you like to be called that?"

"Oz?"

"Ozzie?" she asked, giggling.

"Sounds like dizzy," he said.

She laughed again.

"But Osborne's better," she said. "More dignified."

"What's digni—?"

"Fancy. Classy."

"I don't know."

"Of course you don't," she said softly, giving him a hug. "How could you?"

Oz—

Ozzie—

O. C.

Osborne . . . *Osborne!!*

Marty's eyes opened abruptly and he came up on his elbows. "DAD!" he hollered.

CHAPTER
ELEVEN

Saturday afternoon was ideal for track, for running, for regions. Once again, the Salukis stayed right on course, the expected winners in event after event, methodically coming through with only one unfortunate twist. That occurred in the high jump, where Southwestern's Gary Reese turned his ankle on his third and last attempt at the winning height. Even though he nearly cleared the bar, it finally toppled from the standards, and Reese slipped to second place. Luckily, his injury was minor and he still qualified for the state meet.

Marty didn't spend all of his prerace time as a spectator but sought out a remote corner of the college stadium and began putting himself into the Mood—"Race-Readiness" he called it today. He sat, elbows on his knees, head resting in his hands, visualizing himself running away from the pack and crossing the finish line, breaking the tape alone. He reviewed the pain factors, trying to prepare himself mentally to deal with the most difficult physical moments of the run.

Next, he did his warm-up stretching, not losing any of his concentration. When he finally heard his event called, he took off his sweat suit and walked onto the track still loosening up his arms, shaking his hands, twitching his thighs, twisting this way and that. He spotted Harper and smiled when he saw him. During all of Marty's prerace imaginings, Harper had never come into the mental picture. Marty tilted into the start wondering if that omission was a good or bad omen. Before he decided, the crackling snap of the starter's gun sent them all scurrying down the track, hustling for position around the first turn. Marty and Ted Harper moved quickly into the lead.

After one lap, two other milers were still close enough to challenge for the qualifying spots. The pace was very fast, wicked in fact. Down the backstretch of lap number two, Ted Harper took the lead and began building distance between himself and Marty. All the runners held their positions through the third lap.

At the start of the fourth and final lap, however, Marty made his move, he hoped not prematurely. Coming out of the first turn he closed in on Harper, and the two of them soon left the others far behind. It was now, typically, a two-man race. Halfway down the backstretch Marty took the lead, which he held until the last turn. But as they rounded the final curve, Harper pulled even.

In what was later described by one sportswriter as "the most perfectly choreographed dance of determination imaginable," Marty and Ted raced furiously down the home stretch, matching stride for stride. The crowd, on its feet, screamed rhythmic encouragement—Sa-LUUUUU-kis!! Sa-LUUUUU-kis!! Coach Hiles at trackside hollered along with all the other idle members of the team. Neither one of the milers was able to muster enough of a final kick to put away the other; each of them dove for the tape at exactly the same instant, using exactly the same form, challenging the eyes of the finish-line judges, who were caught without "photo-finish" equipment.

The official on Marty's side of the track, the inside, thought Marty had won; the judge on the outside gave it to Harper; the judge in the press box couldn't decide who'd won; so for the first time in region-track history, the mile run ended in a dead heat, actually a very live heat, both racers coming in only a few seconds off the region record.

Following their plunges at the finish line, Marty and Harper were both banged up. Hiles was ecstatic, however. He and his region-winning team were going to enter the state meet with not one, but two region-champion milers.

It was also on Saturday afternoon that Detective Eldon Taggert got his first break. When Marty returned home with his father from regions, Taggert was there waiting.

After Taggert congratulated Marty, he said, "You dream good."

Marty looked at him quizzically. "I don't get it," he said.

Taggert said, "I spent my day visiting tennis clubs in town. At the last one on my list—isn't that typical!—I found a guy who was once an assistant manager at the old Metro Tennis and Racquet Club. The guy remembered O. C. very well. Said he was an assistant pro there. Best of all he could identify Stacy from a series of ten pictures of different girls. He remembered seeing them together a lot. He also told me that, yes, O. C. was a real playboy type. Yes, he did live somewhere out near Lake Minnetonka. Yes, he did coach part time at some high school. And yes, he was about to be fired."

"What for?" Marty asked.

"Guess."

Marty shook his head.

"For hustling too many of the married women and their daughters who were supposedly taking lessons from him, for dealing to the kids, for falsifying his time cards. Lotsa stuff."

"So it's true, all of it," Marty said. He sat down carefully, stared at the floor.

"Probably. But we still have a lot to prove. And even if we can prove it all, we still need O. C. alive and well to charge him."

"What'd you mean before about dreaming?" asked Marty.

"This manager remembered O. C.'s whole name. Curt Conley. You wondering why O. C.?"

Marty thought a moment. "Because his first name was—"

"You got it," interrupted Taggert. "Osborne. Osborne Curtis Conley."

Well, there you are, thought Marty.

"You got any other good evidence hiding in your subconscious?" The question was out before Taggert realized what he'd said. "Sorry," Taggert mumbled.

Marty shrugged. "That's it, though," he said. "I mean, that's what she was yelling, right?"

"Maybe," said Taggert. "'No-Gee-Skurd' could have been 'O. C. Curt,' and she never got to the last name. That's my guess."

"Anything else?" asked Ken.

"Oh, the best is yet to come," replied Taggert, snapping a manila folder from his clipboard. "You'll love this."

"Yeah? Why?"

"Seems our boy Osborne Curtis Conley has been doing things. He's got quite a sheet on him. Listen."

Marty sat quietly as Taggert rattled off the list of O. C.'s arrests. Some of the charges included driving while intoxicated, disturbing the peace, possession of a controlled substance, vagrancy (New Mexico); petty larceny—bad checks, loitering, possession, two D.W.I.'s, resisting arrest (Arizona); debauchery (Texas); conspiring to sell controlled substances, indecent liberties, D.W.I. (Minnesota); contributing to the delinquency of a minor, pandering, D.W.I., menacing assault—phone threats, careless use of a motor vehicle, petty theft, possession, disorderly conduct, firearms violation (California); and so on.

"You want it all?" asked Taggert, looking up from the list. "Don't wanna bore you."

"Why isn't he in prison for five hundred years?" asked Marty.

"He's done a little time. The guy's a champ at copping pleas, apparently. Gotta give him credit. He never stays put for long. None of this is real heavy-duty stuff. No aggravated assault, no major felonies. He just sort of slips and slides through the system. Let's see, maximum time served was three months minimum security in California."

"He gets around," Marty said.

"That's what we're looking into now. His patterns. He seems to move pretty regularly. Follows the warm weather. Looks for jobs. Runs from the law."

"Does he find work?" asked Ken.

Taggert said, "The boy's still good at racquets."

C H A P T E R
TWELVE

During Southwestern's last official week of existence, things heated up. Outside the afternoon temperatures hit a humid ninety while inside the students languished for lack of air conditioning. "Closing week" was usually a challenge for the administration and staff because it was the seniors' last chance to be silly, irreverent, irresponsible kids. So a certain amount of food fighting, firecracker throwing, smoke-bomb lighting, class cutting, on-campus drinking and smoking, and gross defacing of school property was expected. Expected, not tolerated.

This Monday, however, the seniors were too hot to move or talk, let alone revolt and disrupt. Like everyone else, Marty dragged himself through the day. Sixth hour, however, he was thrilled to learn that pragmatic John Hiles had shortened practice to "individual stretching" rather than risk losing someone to heat exhaustion. The state meet was Saturday, but unless the weather changed dramatically and quickly, training for it and running in it would be pure torture, not the triumph they sought.

After school Marty was free to leave, and he did. He would do his stretching at home, in the cool comfort of his rec room.

"This is no way to live," Harper said as they walked out of the building into the oppressive stillness.

The moment Marty got home, he snapped on the air-conditioner, shut all the windows, and flopped, exhausted, on his bed. He closed his eyes and drifted off, sleeping soundly, hearing nothing until his father said, "Wake up, Marty. Time for another summit. You eat yet?"

"What time is it?"

"Six."

"No."

"Really. It is," said Ken Oliver, holding up his wrist, showing Marty his watch.

"I mean no, I haven't eaten yet."

"Oh. You want pizza? We need to get something fast."

"Why?"

"Taggert and Hiles are coming over again. Eldon thinks he has something."

"No lie?"

"Unh-uh. Look, you shake out the cobwebs. I'll get supper."

Marty stuffed himself shamelessly with the thick, spicy pan pizza. He was so dulled by overindulgence he was ready for another nap just as the meeting started. Instead, he fought to keep his eyes open while Taggert plodded through his report.

Finally, Marty's dad spoke up. "So the guy gets around, Eldon. So what?"

"Can't you see it, Ken? The boy seems to have a fairly regular travel schedule."

"I'm still lost."

"Where was he three years ago?"

"Here. The Twin Cities. You just documented that."

"Six years ago?"

"Here . . ."

"Nine years ago?"

Ken's eyes glowed with comprehension. "You think he's here now, don't you—the rule of three's or something?"

Taggert said nothing, but gave a small nod.

"Wait," said Ken. "If he's done what we think he's done, why would he come back here?"

"Why not?" replied Taggert. "Everywhere he goes he eventually wears out his welcome. The boy can't stay out of trouble."

"But why here? Why not Chicago? Cleveland? Boston?"

"He's got friends here, maybe a part-time tennis job, a setup."

"So get him," Hiles suggested.

"And charge him with . . . what?" asked Taggert.

"The kidnapping of Stacy Davis, maybe her murder," said Marty's father, his voice tight with irritation, anger. When there was no quick nod from Taggert, Ken asked, "What's the problem?"

"I'm surprised at you, Ken," said Taggert. "I've got an uncorroborated, unsubstantiated, uninvestigated witness, a journal that as far as we know could have been written by anyone—"

"You're saying we have to sit and watch?" interrupted Ken.

"The guy's got no reason to be nervous. We need him to give us something."

"What's the use?" said Hiles. "We don't even know if he's actually here, right?"

Sullen, Marty sat with his fists and jaws clenched. He couldn't believe how close they were, how angry he was.

"I think I can finally see why we're here," said Ken Oliver.

"Why?" asked Taggert.

"You want to give him a chance to incriminate himself, roust him."

"Could be," Taggert said, winking.

Then out of the blue Ken asked, "Are there any big tennis tournaments in town right now?"

"If you quit the newspaper, Ken, you can work for me," said Taggert.

"What's that mean?"

"You're thinking like a cop. The Midwest Junior Open starts tomorrow. It's played here every three years."

"Really?"

"So?" Hiles said.

"So it could be coincidence, but Mr. O. C.'s got perfect attendance."

"What I'm thinking is," continued Ken, "since O. C. has a reason to look at the sports section, why not sneak in a 'staff written' article that might rattle him."

"About what?" asked Taggert.

"Marty and the state meet and the discovery of Lisa Walker's letter."

"Hold it," said Taggert, his face pinched. "Use your son here as bait? C'mon."

"The focus won't be on Marty but the journal. O. C. might think he knows where it is, right? Didn't Stacy mention that O. C. knew she kept it in the garage? But we know where it is now, and what it actually says."

"Invite him to go for it, huh? Hands in the cookie jar?"

"It's worth a try. Either way, he makes a move and we can follow him."

"Either way?"

"He'll either try to find the journal or he'll take off."

"If he bothers to read the paper."

"It's worth a try. Marty?" said Ken, facing his son. "Is that okay with you? Want to risk it?"

"Sure," Marty said.

"Just a minute."

Marty watched his father get up and hurry out of the room. He disappeared into his office. Seconds later, they heard his typewriter.

"Instant analysis," Taggert joked, chuckling.

The three of them sat quietly for the eleven minutes it took Ken Oliver to compose and type the story.

"Here," he said, coming back into the family room. "It's not long, not great, but it should do. It's credible." He handed the single sheet to Marty first. It read:

OLD NIGHTMARE STILL HAUNTS
STAR MILER

No, Southwestern's Marty Oliver isn't bedeviled by the thought he might lose someday. He knows that possibility always exists. He also knows he has the inside track statewide in his event this year.

No, what disturbs Marty Oliver these days is a harrowing experience he survived as a five-year-old. Nearly twelve years ago, on a cold October night, his baby-sitter was kidnapped while Marty slept unharmed, upstairs. Ironically, the baby-sitter, Stacy Davis, was also a talented distance runner at Southwestern where she worked with John Hiles, who is now Oliver's coach.

The case of her disappearance remains unsolved. She was never seen after that night, and authorities suspect she was murdered by her kidnapper. But her memory haunts Marty Oliver. "It's something I think about a lot," he said. "Sometimes I imagine she's still alive and that she'll come back here and explain everything. It's tough sometimes."

It's been tough for local law-enforcement agencies as well. "There was no useful evidence found at the crime scene," said Detective Eldon Taggert. "We've never had a suspect. And nothing's turned up during the intervening years to change that, until now."

What encourages Taggert and troubles Marty Oliver was the discovery this week of an unopened letter written twelve years ago. It was found by Coach Hiles, who explained, "Because this is our last year [Southwestern is scheduled to be closed in June], we've been carefully going through the file cabinets and deciding what to keep. The letter was stuck between two folders. I'd never seen it before."

And the contents of the letter? "The writer is anonymous," said Taggert. "But obviously it was some friend of Stacy's, a close friend. There are hints in it that Stacy kept a detailed diary or journal, which apparently is still hidden, still safe, just waiting to be found. We haven't located it yet, but we're getting close. The journal should contain information that will warrant reopening a full-scale inquiry."

As for Marty Oliver, he is now preparing to face the rigors of state-championship competition. For him the discovery of the letter is a mixed blessing. "I just want it to end," he said.

When everyone had read the article, Taggert asked, "And what if he doesn't see it?"

"We'll run it, wait a few days. You watch the house. If it's business as usual, we'll try something more direct."

"Like?"

"Like we'll cross that bridge . . ." Ken Oliver waved off the rest of the cliché.

"Ken, we can't spare any personnel to stake out the house full time. I can ask for volunteers."

"It won't be dangerous."

"It won't?"

"O. C.'ll go for the garage if what Stacy said is true. Since the place is empty, can't you just put somebody inside the house? Have him call in if O. C. shows up?"

"The phone's probably disconnected."

"Can you promise a regular drive-by?"

"I'll check. It's all a little farfetched."

"Look, we can't just diddle this away."

"Ken," said Taggert, obviously struggling now to sound patient, "the guy hasn't read the article yet."

"Yeah, okay. The odds are a little stiff."

"One in a million?" suggested Taggert.

"C'mon."

"Worse?"

C H A P T E R
THIRTEEN

Ken Oliver was able to run the story. Tuesday morning, Marty opened the sports section and saw himself squinting at the camera. They'd printed a picture of him with the article, a shot taken after he'd won the conference championship.

"What do you think?" his father asked.

Marty said, "Well, there it is."

Marty expected to get teased about the story at school, but nothing was said all morning. Instead, nearly everyone talked about the weather. Another scorcher was building and classrooms were stuffy and still by third hour, the humidity nearly nauseating. By now, all of Marty's teachers were reviewing for the final exams scheduled Thursday and Friday. Mr. Warner was no exception.

With his forehead perspiring, his light blue, button-down, short-sleeved shirt darkening at the armpits and between his shoulder blades, Mr. Warner gamely attempted to bring the semester into focus.

He began class by holding up a green "administrative memo," pinching it between his thumb and forefinger, scowling as though it were a dead rodent.

"What were we supposed to do today?" he asked the class, still staring at the memo.

"Review," said Gretchen Thomas. "Prepare for the final examination."

"Boooo," mumbled Putman.

"Review for what?" Warner asked.

"Friday's final!" half the class chanted back, Marty among them.

"Will it do us any good?" Warner wondered aloud.

"I don't think so," said Eddie Binelli. "It's too hot to concentrate."

"And why should we?" continued Warner, looking again at the green memo. "Why should we worry about clear, forceful writing and thinking when even if we could master them, we'd be unappreciated, if not ignored."

"What are 'we' talking about?" asked Barry Miller.

"Listen to this," said Warner. "This prose treasure came from someone in charge of communication at this school."

"Who's that?"

"The *Man!*" Warner snapped sarcastically, pointing in the direction of the Office. His flash of sacrilege earned him a decent laugh. "Now listen carefully while I read, and please get a vivid impression of what's accepted as meaningful writing by someone who's getting paid way too much of the taxpayers' hard-earned money. And I quote:

Dear Staff Member:

"A nice personal touch," commented Warner.

As the final curtain falls on our last campaign in Southwestern's long and distinguished road to educational excellence, I want to get the ball rolling, so to speak, on a major people-oriented project proposal that is to be, and will be, funded by the district office. What I want your help in doing is to assemble a working paper list of all present and past staff members whose personalities and good work has—

"That's 'has' mind you," interrupted Warner.

. . . has impacted so significantly on our most critical educational goals and objectives. What we (*your* administration) would like to do is sponsor and prepare and serve up a farewell breakfast during our final workshop day. What we need from you is the names of any and all faculty members (everybody can think of a couple/three), past and present as I said, for we want to develop a master list of all our old teachers broken down by age and sex.

The class erupted with laughter.
"I guess either one of those will break us all down sooner or later," said Warner.
The laughter died.
Marty thought of Stacy, broken by . . .
"So tell me," Warner continued, "how many of you think I'm paid to teach you something?"
To Marty, as to all the other members of the class, this question seemed absurd, the answer obvious.
"Sure you're supposed to teach something, only not so boring," replied Brian Putman.

A few students near him snickered uneasily. Marty tensed at the insult. Warner, however, remained calm, unperturbed.

"Boring. Is that what you said, Brian? I know you're not trying to hurt my feelings, so why would you say something like that?"

Putman offered no reply.

"I'll tell you, then. Would that be better? It's because this class is boring. Tedious, exacting work done to master any difficult activity is often boring. But don't worry about that. Like everything else we do here in English 12, it's all part of a bigger plan. You see, since life in this country is, for the most part, routine and boring, we at Southwestern High School consider English as a means of preparing you for life. For what truly awaits you out there. So, once again, let me pose the question: Am I getting paid to teach you anything?"

"What's the point, Mr. Warner? We're all sufficiently mystified," commented Eddie Binelli.

"The point is," said Warner, as he walked over to the door and eased it shut, "the point is—today I'm going to do something I've wanted to do for the last ten years, something I've never done for anyone before. I want to tell you the Truth, as I see it.

"Sadly, the truth is I'm clearly *not* getting paid to teach you anything. What I am getting paid for is Minding the Store, Carrying On, Perpetuating the Process, while making sure that you harm neither yourselves nor our fine facility here, our beautifully oiled Processing Plant.

"Let me put it this way: If I were getting paid to teach you something, then the amount of my salary would depend on how much you learned, right? Consider people in sales, the authentic ones, the ones living solely on commissions earned. They don't make a dime unless they sell, sell, sell. They don't get paid simply for Trying Hard or for Minding the Store. But here things are . . . quite different."

Marty gave a small coughing laugh.

Gretchen Thomas spoke up. "But if a teacher doesn't do anything, teach anything, can't the administration fire you?"

That question, Marty noticed, brought more emotion into Warner's voice.

"Who among those stooge executives has the courage to fire anybody?" Warner let the question hang in the air.

"Lots of you," he continued, "have, I'm sure, complained about bad teachers. Why are there bad teachers in so many classrooms, you've wondered, when it seems entirely possible to have excellent ones in every classroom. If you don't know why, I'll tell you. It's because such teachers were hired by greater failures than themselves. Think about that."

Marty thought about Bruce Skuppers—principal—and understood.

"But there are two sides to every coin," Warner added. "And by that I mean our administrators are not merely ill equipped to dispose of ineffective teachers. They're at least as poor at recognizing and encouraging and rewarding creative ones. Let's face it. We're not teachers anymore, those of us who have stayed with the public schools. We're civil servants, and damn well-paid ones too."

Marty sat there smiling, taking it all in, thinking of how much his mother would enjoy herself if she were with him now. In Mr. Warner she had a kindred spirit, a Soul Brother.

"What I really mean to say is, I think you're getting out

---

of this prison just in time. And it is a prison. It only runs as well as it does because you let it. As staff members, we're obviously and hopelessly outnumbered, so we need the cooperation of our victims to survive, especially during closing week. I just hope it's not too late for some of you, that we haven't kept you here too long. I hope we haven't killed all your natural energy and creativity and imagination.

"And I hope it's not too late for me. I put myself in this cage with you willingly. No one made me go into teaching. I wanted to do this. But I shouldn't have stayed this long. I should have gotten out years ago. I can see now that the system has been deceiving me almost as much as it's deceived you, little by little, year after year, but fooling me all the same. This is a young person's profession. Maybe they're doing me a favor by closing this place down and laying me off. At least I'll be out, free.

"Do you understand?" he asked with emotion. "We're in the same boat. We have to decide who we are. We have to act. And because hardly anybody wants to go out and *do* things, make things happen, we all run the risk of becoming storekeepers, sitting and waiting for life to find us."

That comment hit Marty like a solid right jab. Suddenly everything Warner had said seemed directly applicable to Marty's situation. Like Mr. Warner, Marty had been frustrated by something for a long time. Like Warner, he'd been victimized by people who'd set up a scene in which he had no role. The school board and central administration had banished Warner, while Taggert and Marty's own father had exiled him. He was alone in it now, and angrier than he'd ever been.

He hated what he had learned about Stacy. He hated the man who'd helped her destroy herself, maybe even killed her. Mostly he hated being afraid and feeling powerless. He realized that *his* time *must* come. Whatever the consequences, he had to *do* something to resolve the matter, not just sit passively by and allow O. C. to escape. So Marty vowed not to let him get away, not to let him slip between police patrols. He vowed to catch O. C. in the act himself.

For a few moments Warner stared at the floor, his mind seeming to wander, looking, perhaps, down the dusty corridors of memory to a time when he was young and naïve and enthusiastic and full of purpose.

"Now what?" blurted Putman, bringing Warner out of his reverie and back to basics.

"Now I want you to take out a half piece of paper, put your name on it, fold it once, and put it in this box."

Marty was amazed at how quickly Warner could shift gears. It was almost as if Putman's question were planted.

When everyone in the room had complied with Warner's request, Eddie Binelli thought to ask, "Why'd we do this?"

"Because now it's time to draw for the Automatic 'A'."

"What'd he say?" asked Putman, suddenly alert.

"The Automatic 'A.' It goes to the name I pick. An 'A' for the entire course."

"But Mr. Warner," whined Gretchen Thomas, "that's not fair! Some of us have worked hard all year to earn a high grade."

"What if you win, Gretchen?" asked Warner.

"Well . . ."

"This is just another lesson in life," Warner clarified. "It's part of the Truth, that Master Plan I was telling you about."

"What part?" asked Binelli, smiling. "What's the point?"

"That sometimes it's better to be lucky than good," replied Warner, as he reached into the box. "But don't worry," he added. "For those of you who don't come up a winner here, we have the Public Assistance 'D −' Option. As soon as I'm done with this, you can apply for a 'D −' by pleading your case before the class. If their applause is sufficient, you've passed. This is a merciful program. You must all have prizes."

By afternoon it was a legitimate ninety-two degrees outside, and inside the old, poorly ventilated rooms of Southwestern High School the air had turned stale, then foul, and students in Marty's social-studies class began voicing their discontent.

"Somebody get an ax and put a window right here," said Gayle Barnes, a cheerleader wearing a powder blue tank top and matching silk running shorts. She pointed to the expanse of plaster wall in back of her.

Some teachers brought fans from home, but they proved ineffective. By sixth hour, Marty was sure that Hiles would have to call off practice again.

"How about it, Coach?" Marty asked as Hiles came into his office.

"You're early, and a little too anxious not to work out."

"I'll run, if you tell me to."

"Let's talk about it. Did you like the article?"

"I guess."

Hiles nodded. "How's this? For practice you take a few laps, maybe go a hard half mile at the end."

"Okay."

"I won't be out for a while." Hiles glanced at his watch.

"How come?"

"You haven't heard."

"Unh-uh. What?"

"Harper. He did it again."

"He's in trouble? He said something?"

"Got smart with Miss Morgan."

"Algebra Two?"

"That's it," said Hiles.

"What'd he say?"

"I don't know the details yet. I'm meeting with both of them and Skuppers right now. Wish me luck, for old Ted's sake."

"Shuttle diplomacy," said Marty. "Good luck."

After Hiles left, Marty asked around until he got the story. Apparently, in Miss Morgan's fifth-hour class, Harper began moaning, hyperventilating, faking heatstroke. Miss Morgan told him to "knock it off and get serious." He responded by rolling up his sleeves and unbuttoning his shirt. Then he pulled his pants legs up and over his knees and kicked off his shoes. He looked like a displaced Caribbean beachcomber. It wasn't long before several slavish imitators around him did the same.

Soon the girls sitting nearby started laughing loudly enough to distract those students seated in the front of the class. When they too began turning around, looking for the cause of the amusement, Miss Morgan reacted. She stood up, slammed a book down hard on her desk and yelled, "Dammit, Harper, pull down your pants and get to work!"

Harper jumped up, bug-eyed. The class exploded in raucous laughter. Miss Morgan's face reddened as the implications of her order became clear. Harper said, "You mean it?" Then he added, self-destructively, "You say where and I'll be there!"

Miss Morgan screamed back, "GET OUT! GET THE HELL OUT!!" Then she marched over to the intercom, buzzed the principal's office, and asked for assistance in removing Harper from her classroom.

"Hey, let's relax, huh?" said Harper, suddenly aware of what he'd done, what it could lead to: a hardball session with the administration, trouble, a suspension, not competing in the state meet. "Look, Miss Morgan," he said respectfully, "I'm turning myself in." He walked toward the door with his forearms up, his wrists ready to receive the handcuffs. That got him another laugh.

And caused Miss Morgan to charge. She rushed at Harper and pushed him into the hallway, right into the waiting arms of Norm Hecker, vice-principal.

Marty left school that afternoon sincerely hoping that Hiles could save the Shadow one more time.

Marty was home alone Tuesday night. He knew he would be. His dad was downtown attending some kind of seminar, lecturing there. He said he'd be late, maybe even stay the night at the hotel.

It was during supper that Marty started to think. Warner's plea kept coming back, rising up, challenging him. *Do something . . . do something . . . make it happen.*

Marty hurried through his meal, cleaned up after himself, and went to his room. He pulled his old sleeping bag out of the closet and set it on his bed. Next, he found the bug spray among the clutter covering the top shelf in the linen closet. He stuffed the little plastic bottle into his jeans pocket. He'd also put on the darkest shirt he could find, a maroon "Southwestern Track" practice jersey. Again he turned to his closet. On the floor in back he discovered his Little League baseball bat, a Louisville Slugger. Seeing it, Marty smiled. He'd been a very weak hitter. That was why the bat remained unmarked to this day. "Swing level! Swing level!!" his father had chanted day after day that summer. "Don't chop, don't reach. Just swing level." But it wasn't Marty's game. Now, however, the bat might come in handy if he found himself in trouble.

Marty left home at dusk and headed for Stacy's old house. He felt self-conscious carrying the sleeping bag with the bat rolled up inside it, but he knew he'd be able to hide himself completely in the park across the street from Stacy's. He strode purposefully toward his destination, trying to cut the ten minutes of walking time in half.

The park offered him a nearly perfect hideout and vantage point. Within sight of Stacy's house, five large blue spruce grew in a circle so tight that their branches intertwined. With his head, neck, arms, hands, and ankles covered with insect repellent, Marty was able to burrow under the thick canopy of boughs and roll out his sleeping bag on the soft, clean bed of brown needles beneath. Watching through the low-hanging branches, yet concealed by them, he had a clear view of the brick colonial where Stacy once lived. Marty was close enough to read the company name on the real-estate sign on the front lawn. Fifteen minutes later it was dark, the only brightness coming from a dim streetlight in the next block. Bugs whined around Marty's head but none bit.

While Marty kept an eye on the house, he began to contemplate his actions. He knew his father would be angry with him, crazy angry, if he ever discovered this covert operation. He would holler about taking worthless, useless risks, he would scream about *common sense!* Marty had seen him like that only three or four times. That was enough.

But so what, he thought. Marty was tired of sitting and waiting for adults to solve his problems. He was fed up with being a victim—of the crime, of his dreams, of official indifference. He was horrified to think his father's well-laid plan might not work just because the police couldn't afford a stakeout. O. C. was guilty. Marty knew it. And Marty would be there when O. C. proved it. He'd confront him, make him admit everything, then threaten to take the man's head off if he tried to get away. Marty felt for the bat, gripped it, his stomach tight with anticipation. It was time to *do something*, and he'd deal with his father's disapproval later. Marty was still imagining dialogues with O. C. when he dozed off the first time. There hadn't been much to see, only a few cars.

It was the bad muffler that woke him. He shoved away the protective sleeping bag, his face sweating in the close, still air. He blinked wildly to adjust to the deep darkness, spotted the rusty Volvo sedan parked in front of Stacy's. Squinting at the car, he reached for the bat. He couldn't see anybody inside.

He wriggled free of the sleeping bag and crawled to the edge of his hideout, dragging the bat with him. Quickly, quietly, he slipped out of the branches and moved in on the Volvo. Crouching, staying in the shadows made by the towering elm, oak, and maple trees scattered before him, Marty worked his way closer to the street. He hid behind another spruce and waited, watched.

Finally, the driver's side door creaked open and Marty's breath caught in his throat. His heart began slamming against his ribs and he sweated profusely. He wiped his lips with the back of his hand and readied himself. The man climbing from the car, dark haired and tall, was halfway out when Marty began circling wide to cut him off.

But Marty stopped short, just two steps from the street, as the other door opened and a young blond woman stepped out holding a folded newspaper and road map. He was caught in the open, a loping lunatic with a Louisville Slugger.

"This is it, Gene," said the woman in a whiny voice. "I told you we should've turned back there. I wish we could've seen it in the daylight."

"How much the paper say it is?" asked the man.

The woman, still not spotting Marty, quoted the asking price on Stacy's house, while Marty, panicking, began slowly then quickly backpedaling, zigzagging, searching desperately for cover. He dove behind an oak tree and held his breath, waited. Nothing, no comments, only the grumble of the faulty muffler when the man started the car. Marty let himself breathe, shallowly and quickly at first, then deeply and evenly. He wiped his oily face with his forearm, shook his head, hardly able to believe what he'd nearly done.

At last the Volvo rumbled away. Marty waited a full minute before returning to his outpost. He was scared, tired, embarrassed. He lay on top of the sleeping bag and breathed deeply. Eventually, he fell asleep again. He was awakened just once more before giving up and going home. This time it was a police prowl car moving slowly past Stacy's, flashing a spotlight on the house, scanning the yard, a quick once-over. Marty decided then he could leave. The sky was barely gray. There should still be time to shower and sleep before school started.

The mission's only success was Marty's making it home undetected. His father had stayed downtown. Marty dragged himself into the shower, then crawled into bed. Before conking out he mumbled, "Hay-ull . . ." à la Ted Harper.

CHAPTER
FOURTEEN

For only the second time all year, Marty overslept Wednesday morning. He woke up just ten minutes before his first class was to begin and stumbled out of bed hoping to take only one tardy, an hour's detention. Hurriedly dressed and without breakfast, he raced out of the house, consoled only by his predawn shower. He would be late but relatively clean and fresh.

Outside, Marty stepped into another oppressive morning. The sun was already blood red, and the blanket of humidity that had covered the city for the last two days seemed even thicker and stickier than before.

Twenty minutes later, when Marty walked into the attendance office, rumors were circulating that Skuppers was ready to close school.

With his yellow "late pass" in hand, Marty headed for his physics class. On the way, a few stragglers stopped and silently stared at him. Near the door of the physics room, two sophomore girls pointed at Marty and exchanged fast whispers. Finally, it dawned on him—the article.

And that's how it went for him all day long. Even Putman, who seemed pathologically compelled to make snide remarks to anyone who'd been singled out for recognition, left Marty alone, glanced at him with sullen respect. Marty didn't see Harper until practice after school. He found Ted alone in the locker room staring at the bulletin board, reading Hiles's suggested practice. The coach had considered a "pool session," a swimming workout, but scratched the idea when he learned the temperature at poolside was eight degrees warmer than outdoors.

Marty approached Harper quietly and said, "You're back."

Harper turned, smiled. "Barely," he whispered.

"Beat the rap?"

"Sort of."

"Let's hear it."

"Gotta do some penalty work for Morgan. Write a letter of apology. Detention."

"When? Maybe we can do concurrent sentences."

"You too?"

"I overslept this morning."

Harper's little smile changed slowly into a big grin. In his "mock-country" accent he said, "My-oh-my. You're slippin', boy. What's this world comin' to?"

Marty shrugged, then saw Ted's bright expression change dramatically, his face suddenly full of apprehension.

"What's the matter?" Marty asked.

Ted replied, "I didn't know."

Marty gave Ted a look of inquiry. He wondered what Harper didn't know this time.

"You understand what I'm talking about?" Ted asked.

"Not really."

"That story in the paper. Stacy Davis."

"Oh, that," Marty answered, with a weak laugh, hollow nonchalance.

"Why'd they write it now?"

"Because of the letter, I suppose."

"C'mon . . ."

"What else?"

"Somebody's getting close to something."

"There's probably stuff in that letter—"

"Either it's all in that letter," interrupted Harper, "or they've got a lot more than they're telling."

Marty waited a few seconds before replying. He didn't want to seem startled by Ted's insightfulness. Marty asked, "How do you figure?"

"You read the story?"

"Sure."

"It's a tease, right?"

"I'm lost."

Ted looked dubiously at Marty. "You didn't see all the invitations in it to think the end is near?"

"Where are you getting all that?"

"Right from the article!" Harper snapped. "I mean, this cop says there's a journal that'll as much as name whoever took her. They wouldn't print something like that unless they either had the journal already or knew that somebody would lead them to it if they just pushed a little. What, they got a suspect? Listen, I watch lots of TV. I know how these things work."

Marty looked away.

"Level with me, okay?" said Harper.

"You're a careful reader," Marty commented, offering Ted an opening, a chance to press him for more. Marty wondered, should he tell him anything? How could he be sure crazy Ted Harper wouldn't spread it all over school? He couldn't be sure. He'd simply have to trust him.

"Where's the journal? You know, don't you," Ted asked.

"You won't tell anyone. You can't."

"C'mon, talk to me."

"It's supposed to be at her old house someplace."

"But it isn't."

"No."

"Who's got it?"

"The police."

"And there's a suspect?"

"Yes."

"So, what's the game? Covert assistance? Surveillance?"

"You mean us?"

"There you go again. Drop the pose, okay? I'm in, you know? I *see* it, babe. Do the cops already have the place staked?"

Marty nodded. "Sort of. Part time. They say they can't spare anyone full time."

"Any action?"

"No. And this may be our only chance to get the guy."

"So you're ready to take a personal interest?"

"I've always taken a personal interest."

"Sorry."

"You never forget something like that."

"I said I was sorry. Sometimes I quit thinking but keep talking, remember? Ask Miss Morgan."

Marty smiled. "Just so you understand. This isn't some screw-off number."

"Whadya want? A note from my mother? I'm sorry, okay? I believe you. It's been hell."

"It is."

"You been at it already?"

"What?"

"Whatever. Keeping watch?"

"Coupla nights, yeah," Marty said, exaggerating needlessly.

"And?"

"Nothing. No slowdowns. Hardly any traffic at all." Marty was about to tell Ted how he'd nearly charged an innocent house hunter last night, but he saved himself the embarrassment.

"I'll be there with you tonight," Harper said.

That night, with Ken Oliver still downtown, Ted and Marty set up camp under the clustered spruce trees. Marty asked, "You sure you wanna do this?"

"It'll be kicky. Already is. Nice change of pace."

"I hope so."

They agreed on a duty schedule, Ted taking the first watch. Again, the sticky night air made sleep uncomfortable and sporadic at best. Yet, like dedicated professionals, they kept their vigil, quietly changing off every two hours. When Harper woke Marty for the last watch, he said, "You're lonely, this ain't where to be."

"Nothing?"

"Nothing."

And that's how it ended.

"You still call this kicky?" Marty asked before they split to go home and shower, get ready for school.

"It was okay. Really. Teaches you patience."

"I already know patience," Marty replied.

"Teaches you self-discipline, then."

"Know that, too."

"Makes you so angry, every time this 'O. C.' stands you up, you'll be crazy when he shows."

"You think so?"

"You'll see."

"Thanks, Ted."

"For what?"

"Staying out here. Helping."

"Boy, what the hay-ull you talkin' 'bout?" said Country Ted.

"Thanks anyway."

"My pleasure."

"Tomorrow night, maybe?"

"What're friends for?"

CHAPTER
FIFTEEN

Thursday was the first session of final exams. Marty was tired but prepared for the three "formality exercises" he was scheduled to perform. "We have to do this," said Mr. Gadney, his physics teacher. "It's a directive from the board. But think of it as a terminal review. Nobody's trying to prove anything with these, okay? We've been together working hard all year, so one exam won't save or sink you."

Not an inspiring speech, thought Marty, who was greatly tempted to slough off and rely on luck and timing.

Thursday was also the fifth day of the heat wave, although relief was near. That news was little consolation to the struggling scholars of the senior class. While the heat gathered, intensified, and hammered down, windless, stagnant, humid, Marty labored through tests in physics, calculus, and economics. Afterward, only finals in English and Spanish stood between him and graduation.

Following still another abbreviated workout, Marty arrived home just in time to answer the phone.

"I haven't deserted you," said Marty's father on the phone. "Really."

"I know."

"We keep missing each other. Everything going okay?"

"Sure. You were here?" Marty asked, wondering if he'd been missed during the night.

"Around noon today. My fifth change of clothes. Pitting-out something awful. We're about done, though."

"So you'll be home tonight?"

"Maybe. I don't know. I hate to miss working with Taggert, but this conference has inspired two or three new projects. I might hang around a little longer to see who goes for what, check out the opportunities. Anyway, it's a waiting game now."

Marty breathed easier. He'd have to cover for himself just in case his father came home. Marty asked, equivocating boldly, "Dad, is it okay if I stay with Harper tonight?"

"You're done studying?"

"When I'm done, I mean."

"I suppose."

Great, thought Marty. Another easy night of surveillance, easy to start with anyway. Marty wondered how he'd do it were his dad around. Would he still risk the mission? Probably.

"Marty?"

"Huh?"

"You hear me?"

"Sorry. What?"

"Make sure you're not eating junk. Get enough sleep. How were the tests?"

"Hard because it was so hot. It was tough to stay awake."

"I imagine. Any news from Taggert?"

"Unh-uh."

"Okay. I guess we'll have to wait and see. Maybe I'll give him a call later. Be good."

"Bye, Dad."

Marty hung up and began searching for his supper.

An hour later, plied with bologna, bagels, and milk, Marty readied himself for a third night of watching. Once more, he donned his blue jeans and Southwestern jersey. Both smelled of insect repellent. He'd begin the stakeout alone. Harper had promised to be along later.

Marty left his house wondering if Harper would show up at all. He wouldn't blame him if he didn't. Last night had been something less than "kicky." Maybe Ted had seen enough. It would be nice to have Harper there, thought Marty, but as Coach Hiles often said, "Your most important battles are fought alone." Marty was ready to go solo.

Following the procedure he'd established the last two nights, Marty again rolled out the sleeping bag under the circled spruce trees, placing his bat near the front edge of the tenting branches. That way he could grab it as he scrambled out. With everything set, he began his vigil. An hour and two drive-bys later he was asleep.

He woke up when the poorly focused headlights of a car coming straight at him from a side street stabbed the darkness, washing over Marty's hideout and all the open area in between. He awoke abruptly, gasped, held his breath. Tense, his heart beginning to beat more rapidly, Marty stared at the old, dented dark-blue Firebird as it crawled around the corner and down the street, heading toward Stacy's. When it got there it didn't stop. Rather, it sped up and went to the next intersection, where it turned and disappeared. Marty kept his eyes on the far end of the block while he worked his way out of the sleeping bag and up to the edge of his cover. He squinted into the night. Even with the dim streetlight in the next block, it was very difficult to see. There were no lights on in any of the neighboring houses. It had to be very late.

Suddenly, he spotted a pale flickering coming back down the alley behind Stacy's. Running lights. Again the car crept past the house without stopping. The Firebird continued to the end of the alley, where the driver snapped on the headlights and repeated the route. Only this time when the running lights approached Stacy's from the alley, they didn't pass by. The car disappeared behind her house. Marty listened carefully. He couldn't hear the engine. He waited ten seconds, twenty. Nothing. He decided to investigate.

Recalling how stupid he'd felt the night before last when he was nearly caught in the open with his bat, Marty decided to leave it behind. This was only a reconnaissance mission, strictly a fact-finding venture. Cautiously, Marty headed out, anxious for a closer look.

Keeping low to the ground, darting, scurrying noiselessly, Marty moved from tree to tree across the space separating his lookout post from Stacy's house. He tried to mix with the blackest shadows. Finally, it was time to cross the street. For a moment, he couldn't decide whether to sprint or stroll up to the house. Instinctively, he chose to run, and he quickly made his way to the south side of the colonial.

There, flattening himself against the cool brick wall, he edged closer to the backyard. Before Marty could go further, he was distracted by two noisy cars racing down

Stacy's street. He got a good enough look to see that nei-ther was the Firebird. When it was quiet again, he peeked around the corner and stared across the yard at the garage. He found no lights, no car. Either the car was gone, or it was parked inside the garage. Marty sucked in a deep breath, bent double, and raced for the garage, for the high rear window. He slid under it and listened.

Hearing nothing, he rose slowly until, half on tiptoe, he could look inside. The interior was so dark and the window so dirty that Marty could see nothing. He ducked down and began cautiously circling the garage. He relaxed only when he found all the doors still securely locked and the Firebird nowhere in sight. It must have slipped away when the other cars passed by. Marty decided to return to camp.

Marty had just stepped from Stacy's front lawn to the sidewalk when the car lights flashed on, caught him squarely in their beam. He turned spontaneously to investi-gate and spotted it, three houses down—the Firebird. Be-fore he could react, break for cover in the park, the car started toward him, slowly, not hurrying at all. Marty opted for a casual pose. He thrust his hands in his jeans pockets and began walking away from the car, toward the streetlight. The Firebird caught up to him quickly and kept pace with him.

With each step, Marty became increasingly alarmed, haunted. His mouth went dry, his heart began thudding when he realized what was happening. This was it—the dream, the old nightmare, coming to life. He wondered if the dream had been a recollection of something he'd actually seen, or a projection, a vision of something he was destined to see, something he was seeing at that very moment.

Just as Marty reached the streetlight, the driver said, "Hey, Oliver."

Marty froze, turned to face the car, aware he'd given himself away completely. His maroon Southwestern jersey camouflaged nothing.

"Listen Star, gotta minute?" said the faceless voice, deep in the shadows of the Firebird.

"Why?" said Marty.

"We gotta talk, pal. Taggert says so."

"About what?"

"He sent me over to baby-sit this place. Said to watch for you. So c'mon."

Marty saw a hand and forearm appear from the curbside window, beckoning him. "C'mere. I'll run you home. We can discuss it on the way."

The latch clicked and the door started to swing open. Inside, a light came on. Marty didn't know what to do, who to believe. He was afraid of the voice, but more afraid of showing it.

"C'mon!" the driver insisted. "Taggert says."

At that point Marty realized everything the driver had said came straight from his father's newspaper story. He knew he should run, but he wouldn't until he'd seen him, looked him squarely in the eye. Marty took a step closer, bent over, and peered into the car. He saw a lanky, gaunt, dark-haired but balding man in his late thirties wearing a snug yellow Ban-Lon shirt over a slight paunch. His eyes startled Marty. They were hostile, piercing, nervous. "Whadya know?" said O. C., reaching for his jacket on the passenger's seat.

Marty slammed the door and bolted, sprinted for the cage of spruce. O. C. was out his door and breathing down

---

Marty's back almost immediately. The man could still move for a guy going to seed, Marty thought. That's when O. C. dove for Marty's legs, an open field tackle. He mistimed it, lunged too early, and barely got a hand on one of Marty's ankles. Without breaking stride or looking back, Marty raced for his hideout, dropping to his knees and reaching frantically under the tree where he thought he'd hidden his bat. He was still scrambling, thrashing, slapping wildly over the bed of sharp dry needles when O. C. caught up to him, kicked him solidly on the side of the head. The blow stunned Marty. White spots hummed before his eyes.

Panicking completely now, Marty jumped up, lashed his forearm in O. C.'s direction and connected, clipping him across the throat. O. C. grunted, started coughing and gagging, breathing raggedly, swearing. Still stunned and blind, Marty dove for cover, scuttled under the thick boughs, rolled in and right over his lost Louisville Slugger. He hugged the bat to himself and held his breath. He could hear O. C. still groaning, gasping, trying to clear his throat. Then silence.

Noiselessly, Marty moved to the spot where two of the trees touched. Slowly he stood up, slipping carefully through the brushing branches, gripping his bat. He figured that sooner or later O. C. would circle the stand of trees, and when he passed Marty's way, he'd ambush him.

The click that shattered the silence and Marty's self-confidence came when O. C. cocked a gun.

"You want, I'll shoot up the woods here," O. C. said in a raspy whisper. "It's over, boy. You've seen me. And I bet you know what I'm after, huh. Why would you be here otherwise? And if you know . . . You better talk to me. What's goin' on?"

Marty didn't answer.

"You get me mad, boy, I'll really hurt you!"

Marty held his ground, fought panic, kept his patience. He knew where O. C. was, not thirty feet away now, barely out of sight. Marty took a step toward the outside of the spruce circle, just far enough to free the bat, get it on his shoulder, ready for a full swing. O. C. was coming right to Marty now, carefully probing each tree with his gun, kicking carelessly underneath, trying to force Marty out. Finally, Marty saw the darkness shift as O. C. came into view. Marty wanted to charge, but knew he'd make too much noise, warn O. C., give him a chance to react, shoot. So Marty waited just a little longer.

And longer . . .

O. C.'s next two steps took forever. But at last he came close, close enough. Marty eyed the darkness, every muscle tensed. He picked out O. C.'s shadow, set his feet, and whipped the bat around, heaving it full power at his target.

Swing level! Swing level! he told himself. And he thought he had. He connected, not solidly, but tagged O. C. hard enough to make him scream, groan. Hit his shoulder maybe. Broke his arm?

Before Marty could make another move, however, O. C. charged from the blackness, rushed Marty, head-butted him, knocked him into the trees, trapping him in the net of tangled boughs. Marty thrashed about, desperately attempting to free himself. Still coughing, O. C. closed in. Marty expected him to charge again, but he dropped to his knees. Why? Looking for something? The gun?

Then O. C. grunted with satisfaction, breathed loudly, insanely, reached for Marty with the revolver, probing,

---

slashing, trying to pistol-whip him. The darkness was suddenly shattered by—

"Drop it! Drop it!!"

Harper!!!

Marty threw himself forward, right at O. C., kicking recklessly as he came down on him, burying his foot in O. C.'s unguarded gut. O. C. bellowed again, tried to roll away, but Marty stayed on top of him. Ted yelled, "Let'm go! I gotta shot!!"

That brought O. C. up. Panic-charged, he threw off Marty and stumbled away, zigzagging toward the street, his car. Bent double, holding his stomach, lurching, looking back only once at the spruce fortress, at Marty who saw him raise his arm, a flame-wink flashing near his hand. Marty heard the crack of the shot as the bullet zipped past his head, *whunk*ing into the tree behind him. Marty dropped to the ground in total fright.

Harper, his legs spread, holding a gun with both hands, leveling it at O. C., squeezed off a round just as O. C. disappeared inside the Firebird. The rear window went gray with spider-web cracks, a neat hole right in the middle. Harper drawled, "Hay-ull!" and took aim for a second shot.

Before he could get one, O. C. slammed down the accelerator and the Firebird shot forward, fishtailing, barely under control, the tires squealing, yelping horribly.

Marty jumped up, grabbed Ted's arm. "Don't!" he shouted. "That's crazy!"

"C'mon, it's only a pellet gun," said Harper. "Let's not panic."

"I don't care. Get rid of it."

In the distance Marty heard sirens keening, getting closer.

"What now?" asked Ted.

"You okay?"

"Sure. You?"

"Think so . . ."

"Nice timing, huh? Even if I do say so myself. Shadow Man on the prowl, comes through big, huh?" Harper was buoyant.

Marty grunted, felt helplessly faint for a second.

"Marty?" Ted asked cautiously.

"Wha'?"

"Hey, let's move it. We can't be here, and you don't sound so good."

"He kicked me, my head."

"You kicked him, his ass!"

Marty laughed weakly.

"Your sleeping bag still over there?"

"Yeah."

Ted quickly recovered Marty's gear and helped him get away. They made it across the park to Ted's car before the first police arrived.

"That was close," Marty mumbled sleepily as they drove away.

"That," said Harper with conviction and a smile, "was *kicky!*"

By the time Ted pulled up in front of Marty's house, both of them knew Marty had received a concussion, probably a mild one. But Marty also knew he'd confronted the man at last, held his own against him, hurt him, made him suffer a little, though not enough to make up for Stacy's suffering.

Marty thanked Ted for saving him. He struggled up the front steps, still half blinded by white bursts of pain. When

Marty unlocked and opened the front door, a look of disbelief crossed his face. His brows lifted, his mouth hung. He was staring at his father, who glowered back, his hands on his hips.

Ken Oliver stepped up to Marty, put his index finger on Marty's chest and pushed. "What is it with you lately?" he asked with threatening directness. "You got a problem?"

Marty looked down, shook his head.

"You got one now."

CHAPTER
SIXTEEN

"**Y**ou're really a disappointment. Lying to me? When did that start?"

"Lying?" Marty answered, playing dumb, buying time. He touched his aching forehead.

"I called the Harpers to invite them over after the state meet. I asked how you two were doing, and Janis said she was about to ask me the same thing since Ted told her he was staying here. So where in hell have you been?"

That about sums it up, thought Marty. Somewhere in hell.

"I asked you a question," said Ken Oliver, his voice obviously strained with worry and anger, his neck cords tight.

Marty took the only available route at five in the morning. He confessed, told his father everything. When he was done, his dad said quietly and evenly, spacing his words out, "I know why you did it, really. But it's useless to be brave without brains. What you did was stupid. Correct me if I'm wrong, but isn't this guy a suspect in at least one felony, maybe a murder? What are you, out of your mind or something?"

Father and son stared each other down for ten long seconds before the ringing phone broke the silence.

Ken Oliver answered and said, "Yeah . . . I do . . . just now, just came in . . . uh-huh . . . yeah . . ." He made notes on a little tablet next to the phone.

Marty said, "Is it—" but was cut off by his father, who raised a hand to silence him. He took more notes. Then he looked up, found Marty, and signaled him over. "It's Taggert. He knows already, wants to talk to you."

"Hello," Marty said tentatively.

"You're a lucky kid," said Taggert.

"I know."

"It was him."

"Yes, I'm pretty sure."

"He say anything?"

"He told me you sent him."

"Really? Impersonating. That's original. I'll add it to the list."

"That's what he said."

"He was armed, shot at you."

"Uh-huh."

"You shoot back?"

"No."

"There were two shots according to the report, witnesses."

"I didn't shoot."

"Your buddy then?"

" . . . Yeah."

"Ted Harper."

"Right."

"What'd he have?"

"A pellet gun."

"Rifle?"

"Pistol."

"Didn't hit him, though."

"I don't think so."

"Well, I'm not sure what to say, what to do with you guys. I imagine your dad has expressed some concern about your activities."

"That's very true."

Taggert chuckled. "Listen, we're trying to find O. C. right now. When we do, we'll pick him up. He's pretty much told us what we needed to know. So you stay put, understand? We'll get him."

"Okay."

"No more heroics."

"No, sir."

"And if you remember something important, something he said, or if he contacts you in any way, tell me immediately."

"I will."

"Don't you have school today?"

"Yes. Last day of finals."

"Well, behave yourself, rest up for your tests. It's early. And relax. I think he'll stay away from you for now."

"Thanks."

"Put your dad on again, okay?"

"Sure," Marty said, handing the phone back to his father.

Ken Oliver placed his hand over the mouthpiece, said to Marty, "Take a shower, try sleeping." He then brought the phone up to his ear but changed his mind and covered it again. "Marty," he said, "the idea was not to use you as bait, not to risk you that way."

"*I* risked it, okay?" said Marty, trying not to whine. "Can't I help? I mean, it's my problem, right?"

"Hardly yours alone."

Marty looked away, decided to swallow the comeback line he was ready to spout. Instead, he walked to the stairs and climbed them slowly. He felt suddenly exhausted, depleted. Still, no matter how stupid or foolhardy his mission seemed to others, he was glad he'd done it, glad he'd kept watch, faced O. C., took him one on one . . . nearly. Most important, Marty had survived.

For the moment, Marty's confidence was back. He felt sure of himself for the first time since Harper beat him in the challenge race. Even his woozy head was clearing. Marty ended the night's work by doing what he'd been told. He showered, then slept for an hour and a half, getting up in plenty of time to make Mr. Warner's final in English 12. And after that, he took his last test as a senior at Southwestern, a Spanish exam.

Before starting calisthenics that afternoon, the boys' and girls' track teams crowded into a section of the stadium bleachers and waited for Hiles to give his last premeet pep talk. Joining the current teams were over fifty of Hiles's former athletes, a few from his first years of coaching. All had come back to pay their respects. While they waited, a burning, brassy sun bore down on them, making heat waves rise in all directions.

At last Hiles appeared, walking slowly toward the bleachers from the locker room, his head down, staring at his clipboard as he crossed the parking lot. Everyone sat quietly until he arrived.

"I wish . . ." he began, standing before them down on the track, looking up, "I wish I'd thought of something memorable to say here, but at times like this, at the real important times, you either don't have the right words or you use somebody else's words and wind up saying things that have been said a thousand times before and don't mean anything. I guess what I'm trying to say now is, there just plain aren't any words that can express how thankful I am to have been able to work with young people like yourselves all these years. And I'm sorry it has to end."

Then, glancing at his clipboard, Hiles continued, "For practice today, we won't ask you to do much, just warm-ups and a little jogging. We want you to be relaxed and ready to do your very best tomorrow when it really counts. It's supposed to cool off by then. Pray to the god of your choice that it does. Because let's face it, we all know we have a chance to be state champions one more time before they shut us down. So even if there's no future. we can at least make the past happen again, one . . . more . . . time! Can we do that tomorrow? Will we?"

"YES!!" the teams hollered back.

Marty smiled when he saw the fiery, competitive gleam flare to life in the intense blue eyes of John Hiles. Next, Marty joined all the other athletes in giving Hiles a spontaneous minute-long standing ovation. About halfway through it, Hiles nodded, made a word-groping gesture with his hand. Then he pulled his cap low on his forehead, tucked his clipboard under his arm, and walked toward the field. Marty watched as Hiles brushed away the only tears Marty had ever seen him shed.

Following the short, easy workout, the underclassmen and alumni lined the track for the last ritual of the season. As always, Hiles took time to honor his seniors with a special "victory lap." So as the crowd at trackside clapped rhythmically and loudly and enthusiastically, Marty and Harper and the rest of the seniors took their last quarter mile as Salukis around Southwestern's athletic field. Even Harper stayed serious and silent.

After supper, Marty was anxious. It had finally arrived, the ultimate test—the state meet. And that realization hit him like a burying avalanche. He wondered if he'd be able to sleep, if he could regain his calm. He'd recovered more or less from his fight with O. C. The headache and dizziness were gone. And he felt bone tired, predisposed to deep, deep sleep. His mind, however, buzzed and twanged like an overloaded powerline. It unnerved him with frightening images, crippling doubts. When Marty was feeling the most distracted, the call came.

"For you!" his father yelled up the stairs.

"Got it!" Marty hollered down, as he headed for the bedroom extension. "Hello," he said, standing in darkness.

"Phone's probably tapped, so—"

"Huh?" interrupted Marty.

"Shut up! Listen!" growled the voice, a crackling whisper.

"Who is—"

"You're gonna pay, you really are. But just when you don't want to. Keep your eyes open, champ. Maybe you'll finish your race. Maybe not. See if you can find me before it's over."

The line clicked dead.

"Marty!" shouted Ken Oliver, who'd done a little eavesdropping of his own. He came bounding up the stairs. "That him?" he asked.

"Yeah," said Marty, stunned.

Ken grabbed his son's upper arms. "I'm calling Taggert. This is out of hand."

Marty nodded, stood silently watching his father's anxious eyes.

"You've got to rest."

Marty kept nodding.

"You want to take something?"

"I better not."

"Go on then," said Marty's dad. "I'll deal with this."

Marty shrugged, shuffled to his room, closed the door, and locked it.

CHAPTER
SEVENTEEN

That night Marty lay awake in the dark for a long time. He was thinking about all the miles he'd run in practice, in competition, on his own. All that work. All that preparation. Years of it. But now, even though he rested in air-conditioned comfort, he was sweating. Anxiously, nervously sweating. Outside, the wind had picked up and the predicted thunderstorm was grumbling its way closer to the city. He heard the distant booms and he waited.

When the gusts were so strong they rattled oak branches against the house, Marty got up, and ignoring the air conditioning, opened his bedroom window. He knelt before the storm wind and closed his eyes and let his face be buffeted by the rushing, humid air. He began to relax, to meditate.

Soon the wind became cool as the storm organized itself and sent the first random swollen drops of rain splattering against the roof. Marty opened his eyes in time to see the sky suddenly explode with bright snakes of lightning that struck at the horizon. He watched as the oak trees, black with rain, stirred in the wind. Despite the noise, despite the thunder and hammering roar of the rain on the roof, Marty felt his body numbing as he concentrated on one thing, one idea, one goal.

It was not winning. That would take care of itself. If he deserved to win, if he'd paid enough, he would win—it was that simple. It was not that he'd escape unhurt. His fall in the challenge race had upset him, but he didn't envision that happening again, ever again.

It was simply that he wouldn't be scared to face this thing, this biggest challenge of his career, scared to run his hardest, to give the race everything he had just to see if he was really good enough. In short, he prayed he wouldn't be scared to win, to risk it all.

And there would be risks, if O. C. meant what he just said. Marty didn't know what to think. He believed that O. C. could kill, but didn't see why he'd want to kill him. Had O. C. gone completely crazy? Did he really think Taggert couldn't protect Marty at a state track meet? Or was it now just a personal grudge for having survived O. C.'s violence twice. The more Marty thought about it, the more frightened he became.

Eventually, Marty got up, closed the window, and climbed back into bed. As drowsiness began to steal over him, just before escaping into a deep dreamless sleep, he recalled the chant, the ritual:

"Don't . . ."

"Let the . . ."

"Bugs . . ."

"Bite!"

"And if . . ."

"They do . . ."

"Hit . . . Hit . . ."

His sleep was silent darkness, undisturbed.

On waking, Marty discovered a marvelous transformation. Gone was the oppressive, irritating humidity of the last five days, and while the wind was still warm, the violent heat had gone out of it. Marty awoke refreshed and ready. At first he was worried because he felt so peaceful, so fulfilled. He was not anxious at all, not the least bit nervous or tense.

Marty swung his legs over the side of the bed. He got up, stopped in the bathroom, then wandered downstairs. On the kitchen table he found still another encouraging sign, a note from his father. It said:

Marty,

I should have told you about this. I'm still not sure why I didn't. But I called Mom two days ago and told her you made it to the state finals. She was thrilled, so excited by it she decided to fly in this morning. She'll get here in plenty of time to see you run. I had to meet some people for breakfast, but then I'll race out to the airport. We'll be looking for you. About last night, that call, please don't worry. Taggert has someone watching our house right now and he'll follow you to the meet. They doubt very much that O. C. will show up there. If he does, they'll arrest him immediately. Taggert's con vinced it's some kind of diversion.

Good luck!

Dad

Marty smiled. He folded and pocketed the note. Oh my, he thought.

At exactly 9:30 Harper rolled up to the curb in front of Marty's house and honked as his sagging, rusting, bulky Pontiac sedan idled roughly. Marty stepped out the front door, locked it, then jogged down the walk. He climbed into the car and pulled the door shut. Ted Harper stared at him, searching his face for something. Marty smiled back.

"That's what I thought," Harper said.

"What?"

"You're primed."

In the stadium locker room, Marty pulled on his red-and-gold uniform and sweat suit and listened to the banter of his teammates. He wondered if anyone else sensed the guardedness in the voices, straining so hard now to create a mood of calming frivolity. Nobody seemed sure what mood was appropriate or what mood had actually been established. All they knew for sure was they were going about some important business. Today they'd be attempting to win the last state track championship Southwestern High School could ever possibly win. Marty was convinced now it was also the last championship campaign John Hiles would ever direct.

Marty was nearly dressed and had just pulled the fresh socks from his gym bag when he spotted another neatly folded note. He took it out, amazed he'd forgotten to look for it sooner. A couple of times each season, before what his dad considered "key meets," he would send his son inspirational messages. In this one his father had written:

"All a man has is pride. We have all done things for pride that we knew were impossible." (Hemingway)

Marty,

No matter what happens today, you're a thorough-bred. The greatest pleasure I've had in life has been watching you prove it over and over again in all kinds of ways.

Love,
Dad (and Mom)

Marty stood staring at the note, his eyes shiny. He tried blinking back the emotion, but a tear rolled out and slid down his face as he refolded the note and placed it in his bag.

"Know what question I'm really sick of answering?" said Ted Harper from behind Marty, startling him.

Marty waited a second to compose himself before responding. "What question is that?"

"I'm sick of people, guys in school and at work, asking me 'Why do you run? What's the point? You running after something or away from something?' I guess they think asking that makes them philosophers. What do you say?"

"I always tell them it gives me self-respect," Marty replied.

"Hey, that's good. That'd shut 'em up."

"What about you?"

"I say I don't know if I'm chasing something or running away from it until the race ends. Usually I'm chasing something, somebody, this hotshot M. O."

Marty laughed.

"Anyway," Harper continued, "I just want to wish you the best . . . cuz you're gonna need it."

Now Marty searched Harper's face for meaning. Ted's voice had sounded cheerful and he was smiling but not with his eyes. He extended a hand and Marty shook it.

"Same to you," said Marty. "Good luck."

"Let's give 'em a show," added Harper before turning away.

Better us than O. C., thought Marty. He walked out of the locker room hoping that Taggert would do his job.

By the time the announcer had made the last call for the state-championship mile run and Marty and Ted had taken their places at the starting line, it was clear that Southwestern was accumulating the points necessary to be in contention for the team championship. Still, the meet was no giveaway. Southwestern had had to fight for every point it won, and at least five other schools were matching them on the score sheets. There were plenty of events after the mile run, but for Hiles and the Salukis this mid-meet event was psychologically significant. To them it set the tone for the rest of the competition.

Finally, the gun sounded, signaling the start of Marty's last four laps as a high school runner. Immediately the top half dozen milers bolted for the lead, the safest spot during the hectic early stages of the race. Realizing the pace into the first turn was disastrously quick, Marty backed off and allowed some runners to pass him. Unfortunately, as the leaders came out of the first turn, Marty found himself boxed in eighth place. He could not get to an outside lane even if he let the runner on his right move ahead of him, because others were so close behind. Marty chose to be patient. Besides, the pace was as fast as any he'd run all year, so he didn't think it would be wise to push himself so soon.

As they flew down the backstretch, Marty became irritated with the front-runner, who was only an above-average miler but who was willing to sacrifice all his stamina and strength just to be able to say he led the mile run for one or two laps. Such a strategy, however, couldn't be ignored, couldn't be dismissed. Marty remembered watching the state meet as an impressionable eighth grader and seeing Southwestern's mile star that year get upset in the finals by a mediocre runner who, after leading for a lap, suddenly believed he could win, and he did. The Saluki nearly caught him at the tape, but because he'd expected the leader to fade long before the final stretch, he'd allowed him too much distance. Even with a furious final kick, he couldn't make up the yardage. Marty vowed not to let that happen to him.

Suddenly, there it was, his chance to break out of the cage of bodies that had kept him pinned to the inside curve of the track for almost an entire lap. With long, accelerating strides, Marty pulled out and passed the three runners bunched in front of him. Up ahead he saw four more of his competitors, his teammate Ted Harper running in third place. As they finished lap two, the inevitable began to happen. Even before making the first turn of the next lap, the boy who'd led from the start began to drop back. He was passed first by a runner from northern Minnesota, then by Harper, then by the runner between Marty and Ted, and finally by Marty himself. Down the backstretch of lap three, the two boys ahead of Marty began to slow, so that when the race was three-fourths over, the leaders were both from Minneapolis Southwestern, once again. The gun lap, the final lap, began with Harper several strides ahead of Marty, and Marty sneaking two quick sidelong glances at the stands. He was looking for O. C., hoping they'd already caught him.

As for Harper, Marty knew he'd have to catch him much

earlier than he would any other miler. For the last two weeks Ted had proven day after day, lap after lap, that this time things were different, that he'd found and tapped that something extra. Marty couldn't permit him the confidence-building experience of keeping a steady lead for another hundred yards. He decided to make his move.

When he did, when he closed the gap between himself and Harper and ran shoulder to shoulder with him for fifty yards, the packed stands began bellowing encouragement. Down the last and longest backstretch ever, the two runners inspired standing ovations from section after section of spectators as thousands of fans who had no particular loyalty to Southwestern stood up to cheer for Marty and Ted. From the Southwestern rooting section came the infectious chant of "Sa—LUUUU—kis! Sa—LUUUU—kis!!"

Just before leaning into the final turn, Marty reached deep for his own reservoir, that special burst of energy Hiles had told him was always there, would always be there when he needed it most, because of what he was, the Last Goodie. Marty called it up, and it was there, and slowly he pulled away from Ted Harper, who yelled, "GO! GO!!" as Marty forged ahead and began his final kick. His opponent now was the stopwatch.

Coming out of the turn, his legs and arms and lungs alive, afire, Marty knew he could run through it all, that he could ignore the pain. With the chant of the howling crowd reverberating in his ears—"Sa-LUUUU-kis! Sa-LUUUU-kis!!"—he thought about Ted and how his friend had forced him to run the best race he'd ever run at the best possible time, and Marty wondered if Coach Hiles had put Ted up to it, if he'd asked Harper to sacrifice for the sake of a record or a win or something more important, and he knew that if he ever said anything to Teddy about his suspicions—that

Harper had burned himself out so Marty could be great for four laps—if he even said something as simple as "Thanks Ted," Harper would snap back with, "For what?" and Marty would say, "For pushing me," and Harper would put on a goofy lopsided grin and drawl, "Boy, what the hay-ull you talkin' 'bout?" But Marty would know Ted had understood him, and that would be that. . . .

Still, it wasn't all Ted. How could it be? Marty had paid for this championship. He had paid in full for three long years. He had never let up, never compromised, and he was running now to collect on his investment. He didn't know what winning the race would mean to him tomorrow or next month or next year. He only knew that today because of it, because of everything connected with it, his family, his past, their future, that just now it was the most important thing in the world. . . .

So as he neared the tape, with each long, floating, light-footed, light-headed stride, he thought about running after and away. He had seen his mother and father in the third row holding each other, jumping up and down with excitement just before the race had started, and he thought he could hear her calling him home now as he sprinted toward completion, chasing unity . . . of himself . . . for his family.

With his eyes squinted shut—defying O. C.—with a grimacing smile tightening his face, he poured out the last of it, every drop, and knew as he closed in on the finish line, as the screams from the completely ringed infield and crowded grandstands became loud and frenzied, as the world suddenly seemed to move fluidly past him, cut by his slicing, gliding stride, he knew that nothing could make him look back, that he would win, that he'd already won.

"This is for you, Stacy," he murmured. "This is for you."

At the Olivers' "victory barbecue" that evening, Marty had been in the backyard talking to Coach Hiles and his wife when he heard the phone ringing. He excused himself, stepped inside, and answered it, heard Taggert say, "Good news, kid. Put the old man on too, okay?"

"Okay," said Marty. He ran outside and discreetly whispered to his dad, "Taggert's on the phone." The two of them hurried back in, Ken taking the call from his office, while Marty hung up the kitchen extension and raced to the one in his parents' bedroom. Privacy.

"Let 'er roll, Eldon," said Ken Oliver when he heard Marty come on the line.

"We got him."

"O. C.?!" said Marty's father.

"At Stacy's. In the garage. Guy drives right up, comes limping in and goes directly for the attic ladder. Finds the journal up there in two seconds and—"

"Journal? You planted it?"

"Uh-huh."

"You knew he'd show."

"Woulda bet my pension on it. I mean, carrying out death threats just isn't what he does. He can be violent but he'd rather use finesse. He'd rather slide. We figured his threat was a fake."

"What'd you say when he came out with it?"

"'Double fault, sweetheart.'"

Both Ken and Marty laughed. "Good line," said Ken.

"Worked on him too. Course he heard it with a three-fifty-seven Mag. on his nose, might've affected his reaction. And kid . . ."

"Yeah?" Marty said.

"If it's any consolation to you, the man was hurtin'. You boys reached him the other night."

Marty felt good about that, but was too embarrassed to say so.

"Then what?" asked Ken.

"I read him his rights and took him downtown. And you know what he says on the way?"

"What?"

"'I'm glad it's over.' I told him it was over twelve years ago. That he didn't ace just anybody. Then I said he could call a lawyer if he cared to, but first I wanted to talk to him off the record, man to man."

"He confessed? Is that where you're heading?"

"Not exactly. The boy did what I expected him to, though. Offered to cop a plea. He knows the game, the system. So no, he didn't start blubbering and telling all. The guy's not dumb. He did a little probing to see what we had. Pretty soon he wants to play Let's Make a Deal."

"No murder-one, huh?"

"That'd be tough to hang on him, Ken. Probably impossible."

"So? What have you got?"

"Enough. I waved a little of it at him. Reminded him of the journal, mentioned that eyewitnesses are available who can place him with Stacy on numerous occasions, hinted that lots of other strong circumstantial evidence is surfacing. But you know what? The guy isn't weighing and measuring too much. So then I asked him if he wanted to talk about reality. I said we could keep him around until he did because the offenses seem to be snowballing. Mentioned assault with a deadly weapon, breaking and entering, reckless use of a firearm, disturbing the peace, making life-threatening phone calls. All that. Got his attention, and whadya know, he spills."

"She's dead for sure," Marty said quietly.

"Yes," Taggert replied. "I'm sorry. Believe me, Marty, every cop knows a murder takes something from everybody that you never get back."

There was an awkward silence that built before Ken Oliver said, "How did it happen?"

"Says he came to your place that night just to talk to her. Wanted to work things out. But she wouldn't answer the door."

"He's saying she knew he was outside?"

"Right."

"Why didn't she call for help?"

"Sounds like it happened pretty fast. Right away he entered through the basement window. When he met her on the stairs and she screamed, he panicked and hit her, more than once he thinks. He says he lost control. He knows he's sick that way. He didn't know how bad she was hurt. There

---
163

was blood, so he decided to take her out to his car, maybe to a hospital. Instead, he drove west, toward his lake place. By then she was barely breathing, quick and shallow. Sometimes she stopped but then she'd gasp and start up again. He said one pupil was twice as big as the other."

"Cerebral hemorrhage," said Ken.

"She died about an hour after he took her."

"Did he tell you where she's buried?"

"He's saving that till he sees the deal. I asked him if he was sure he remembered where, and he gives me this look and says, 'I'll never forget that.' Anyhow, the bottom line is that we got him and we aren't lettin' go. This boy'll pay, count on it."

"I hope so, Eldon. I really do."

"You wanna hear his best line?"

"Why not?"

"Guy said he loved her, only girl he ever really loved and never knew till it was too late."

"Breaks your heart, doesn't it? Sounds like TV, life imitating art. Eldon?"

"Huh?"

"You've done a helluva job on this one."

"Thanks. You too. And you, kid, you were great."

"Thanks," said Marty.

"You got great timing," Taggert added. "Just as I'm taking him in, the radio sports guy read the results of your race. Congratulations on the record. I turned it up real loud, made sure loverboy got it all."

Before Marty could respond, his father said, "Eldon, will you be able to stay with this one, push the prosecutor a little?"

"What do you think?"

"Mr. Taggert?" said Marty.

164

"What?"

"I really appreciate—"

"Kid," interrupted Taggert, "it's over."

Marty slowly replaced the receiver and looked down from the bedroom window at the party going on below, outside. They were all there, the ones who'd helped the most. There was Ted Harper with his own dad talking to Marty's mother. Hiles was heading toward them. Marty watched his mother smile, shake the coach's hand, and nod approvingly at the trophy Marty had won, a centerpiece on the sprawling, food-laden picnic table.

Suddenly, his mother's attention shifted to the patio doors. Marty looked on as she began walking toward the house. She'd gotten halfway there when Marty's dad, coming outside, intercepted her. He took her gently by the upper arms, leaned close to her, and whispered something. Then he looked around expectantly, perhaps scanning the yard for Marty, glancing finally at the bedroom window, spotting him, then waving to him, both his father and mother, smiling, beckoning now, calling him down to be with them; and at that very moment Marty realized what had happened, what had been accomplished, and he felt a rush of relief unlike any high he'd ever gotten from running, for he knew that finally the ugly beasts of memory that had haunted and terrified him for so long were locked securely in cages at last, and that for this one brief moment, perhaps never again, but for now he could honestly and accurately believe—

I want nothing.

I fear nothing.

I am free.
